For licensing/copyright information, additional copies or for use in specialized settings contact:

# James Colwell

412-322-6464

www.JCNovels.com
Email: jcnovels@msn.com

# Learning Topaz

## a Trifecta

*My Topaz series is dedicated to all those who dare to dream regardless of what limits you've been told that your future holds.*

*James Colwell*

# *Learning Topaz*

## Table of Contents

# What's Next

A mix of emotions ran through my body as I sat on the edge of my bed and looked around my bedroom. To think, I have spent the last year and a half in this space and now my surroundings are getting ready to change yet again. It will be scary but I welcome the experience, moving on to college is another milestone in my life; I've got to succeed, this will pave the way for the rest of my life. I'd become so strong through the turmoil that I've endured in the last few years…

I've fallen into a forbidden love triangle that had a devastating secret attached – and that didn't break me. I've dealt with hate on all levels, in and out of my home - and that hasn't broken me.  Then I felt like

I found the love of my life, only to be betrayed by

him on a deep, deep level - and I'm still standing.

Sometimes I feel as though I am a drama magnet, but I

can take it, I don't know why things seem to find

their way to me in the way that they do, but Mama J

always says, "God puts trials on the folks he knows

can weather the storm!"  When it gets rough I always

hear her speaking that to me and I know that it is my

job to push through whatever little thing that is

making me uncomfortable.  Hopefully some of my drama

will find a different home soon and a little true

happiness may find it's way into my life.

In the midst of my deep thought I heard three

soft taps on the door, I responded, "Who is it?"  Mama

J answered, "It's me Baby, everybody's here and it's

time to get pulled out."  I opened the door and told

her, "I'm ready now."  She grabbed my hand and we

started down the hallway and declined the stairs, as

we reached the front porch, everyone was there to see

me off, Jay-Jay and Quan, Uncle Joe, Whalid, Christine

and Jeremi.  I smiled and said, "Thanks guys, thank

you all for seeing me off, I will be home to visit in

a couple of months, so until then, be good and don't do anything that I wouldn't." Papa J said in a chuckle, "Ha-ha, my son you didn't leave folks much, you don't do anything!" I just smiled, and thought to myself, 'Man, if you only knew!'

We started getting into the appropriate vehicles, Uncle Joe was going to be riding with Mama J and Papa J. Jay-Jay was riding in my jeep with me; Quan couldn't go, he had to be at work in two hours. Christine couldn't go she had plans with her mom, and Jeremi was going to ride with Whalid. As we took our seats I noticed Jeremi and Whalid had gone back into the house shortly after Christine had pulled off. We were all waiting for them to come back out, so our caravan to the college and my new apartment could begin. I realized that I had forgotten my cell phone charger in my bedroom, I jumped out ran past Papa J's window and told him I had to get it and I would tell Whalid and Jeremi to get the lead out. As I approached the porch I could hear yelling, I just took my time and went into the house and proceeded to my room, I had my ear on bionic listening the whole time. Whalid and Jeremi were in the kitchen, Jeremi was going on and on about how he didn't appreciate the treatment and how it wasn't getting any better. I understood where he was coming from, but this really wasn't the time. As I declined the steps, the conversation took an ugly turn, Jeremi yelled, "Fuck you Whalid, and your fuckin' big head ass Bitch, I'm sick of her, I'm sick of seeing her, I'm sick of hearing about the bitch and I'm sick of you chasing the bitch - she don't want you!" Whalid replied, "First of all you don't know what you're talking about, and I've told you before not to insult him, you're the one with the big, muthafuckin' head. And he does want me, we just gotta patch things up, and you should be glad because when things are patched up there won't be anymore you or your mother. So just enjoy the time that you have left with this dick and shut the fuck up you crazy ass hoe." I couldn't believe what I was hearing, after all these weeks, these two are still going through all of these delusions and trials, I refused to even feed in to it, I am over all of it and I want to keep it that way, let them battle it out.

I walked into the kitchen and I watched as Whalid's eyes widened, he was startled, he was so caught up in the ridiculous argument that he hadn't even heard me come in the house. I noticed Jeremi rolling his eyes at me, I played it off and said, "C'mon folks, we've got to go. We have a two hour drive ahead of us." Whalid said, "You're right Baby Boy, let's get going. And anything you overheard, I apologize for." I looked at Jeremi and tilted my head slightly to the right and said, "Hear no evil, see no evil." I began walking out of the kitchen and toward the front door when I heard Jeremi blurt out, "Fuck you, you Bitch - you think you're the shit don't you? But you're not, your brother or whatever he is to you is just trippin', he know he can't replace me with the likes of you. I give him what he needs, it ain't all about being cute and dainty, you fuckin' queen." That was just a bit too much for me to ignore, I was getting real tired of Jeremi, real quick. I responded, "So Jeremi, what is it about? Is it about swallowing cum and eating ass trying to become something you'll never be. That's right, you will never be ME! Period, no matter what little fowl sexual act that you perform will ever put you in the spot of me with Whalid and I don't know why you don't understand that. None of it ever made sense anyway, I didn't do any of that stuff that he has you doing, but you are perfectly suited for what you've got - your mouth is a dumping ground." Jeremi started walking down the hall toward me, I didn't worry nor back down, I made sure I had adequate footing and space around me, I was in no mood for this foolishness this morning. He stopped right in front of me and said, "Just remember, I'm fucking the man that loves you and I guess that's easy to deal with, but is it easy to deal with the fact that I fucked the man that you were in love with, have you gotten over that? There was nothing like seeing you fall to the floor all dramatic when you seen his dick so far in my ass that you thought you were looking at a portrait of yourself. Ha-ha, Bitch that made my day. And by the way how is Ty, I could go for some more of that big ass dick now." I was a little lost for words at that moment, I just turned around and walked out of the house and onto the porch. As I made my way to the porch I heard

Whalid tell him, "Shut the fuck up Bitch, I mean it,
I'm gonna slap the shit out of you if you don't stop."

The two of them came out onto the porch and as
Whalid was applying the locks to the door Jeremi said,
"Whalid, I need some money, I'm not riding with you to
take this Hoe nowhere!  I'm glad to see you go, you
Trick-Ass Bitch!"  I said, "You know what, Whalid
please give this bus-catching bitch fare before I get
really mad."  Whalid was getting the money from his
pocket when Jeremi responded, "Did you always make
sure Ty had bus fare when you were with him?  He
caught the bus over the day that you caught him
fucking me."  A waive of anger came over me in a quick
jolt and before I knew it I had used all the strength
I had and slapped Jeremi's face, he stumbled backward
and by the time he decided he come back at me Whalid
had stood in between us.  Jeremi's mouth had filled
with blood; I said, "Think about that feeling the next
time you decide to put your mouth on something that
doesn't concern you!"  Whalid gave Jeremi the money
and told him to get going to which he obeyed and said,
"We're not done ugly!  I promise you that, we are not
done."  He took off and ran up the street toward the

bus stop. By this time all attention had gone to the action on the porch, Jay-Jay had gotten out of the jeep and was fast approaching as was Uncle Joe. Both Mama J and Papa J were standing in front of their car with a completely puzzled stare as Whalid tried to explain, "It's okay, my two boys had a little disagreement, but they cleared it up. Everything is…" I cut him off, "No! Your little boy had too much to say, which I'm getting real tired of. I'm not going to keep allowing folks to get slick with the lip and get away with it. And for the record, I'm not your little boy, now let's go if you are still going." We began to get back into the vehicles, Mama J looked at me and said, "We will talk about that later Topaz." I responded, "I'd rather not Mama." She said, "But what in the world would cause you to…" Papa J cut her off, "Trudy, whatever it was you know it must have warranted the reaction that he got, that is not Topaz's normal behavior, so let it go Baby, if he wants to talk he will. But I'm glad to see my son sticking up for himself, and as he always says, It is what it is." He chuckled and got into the car, Mama J responded, "I guess your right Wade." To which Papa J nodded in agreement. Uncle Joe then said, "Hey Wade, Man, you really been doin' some work with my nephew. He is changing a lot; not taking shit, I love it! You don't know how many times I watched and had to refrain from killing my family members about bothering him. I didn't think he would ever come out of his shell, which was okay with me, I vowed to God that it didn't matter if he never fought back that I would keep cracking heads about my baby as long as I had breath in my body." Papa J said, "Actually Joe, I only showed our guy a few things physically to protect himself and he seems to have run with them. I know his mouth can be rough at times, he can say some mean stuff on the drop of a dime when his feelings are involved, I believe he gets a lot of that from Trudy." The two men burst into laughter, as Mama J rolled her eyes and said, "He says what he needs to, and I'm glad." Uncle Joe said, "I just can't thank y'all enough for taking and raising him right. And I know I shouldn't laugh but, did you see how he slapped the shit out dude? It's wrong but I was cracking up on the inside, sorry." Papa J chuckled and said, "Hey, It is what it is!"

Whalid very quietly took a seat in his truck with a worried yet relieved look on his face. He was just glad that Jeremi didn't continue to blab and uproot all of his dirt in front of our parents and truly that is part of the reason I decided to crack him in the mouth. He is just so messy and unpredictable, sometimes I think that kid doesn't have it all upstairs. Shortly after we pulled off Whalid sent me a text message that said, "Sorry Boo-Bear," to which I ignored and did not respond.

In my jeep Jay-Jay was patiently awaiting an explanation for all the drama. While on our two hour ride to my new destination I explained, with few details, the reason that Tylique and I were no longer a couple was due to him sleeping with Jeremi. Jay-Jay was in shock; he said, "No wonder you would never talk about the break up, I am so sorry. And you are good, to let that Bitch be anywhere near you and you are just now popping that hoe in the mouth, Baby, she is lucky. I'd have let that Bitch have it a long time ago, and then again every time I see her. I told Quan that I didn't like that sissy, she just looks sneaky; fuckin' Bitch!" I responded, "It's okay, he did me a favor, that's less time that I had to waste finding out about Tylique and his true nature. I was so in love with him, but it seems as though those feelings have turned to hate, the betrayal really got me with that. I have no interest in talking to him or anything, and before that I couldn't wait to be with him. Everything was just perfect, I guess a little too perfect!" A single tear fell from my eye, I refused to give in to the feelings and I just kept driving and changed the subject, "I can't wait to see what my classes are gonna be like, and to meet all these new folks from all over the place." Jay-Jay responded, "I know, and you know I will come up and stay the weekend with you as much as I can, although Quan and I are on a strict budget, we will work it out." I said, "That is so awesome, how is it living together. No parents around or anyone to tell you what and how to do stuff, now it's all your own rules." He answered, "Well, it's still not all my rules, there are two of us, of course you know Quan grew up a completely different way than I did. He had good parents that were good to him and he learned so many things about effectively running a household. So most times I just follow his lead, but he always

listens to my opinion and leaves me room to make

mistakes without getting too frustrated.  Because he

knows my background story, a lot of things that he

thought everyone knew, I didn't have a clue about.  My

mom stayed too drunk and my dad was too busy punching

me to teach me how to be an adult.  I love Quan, I

don't know where I'd be if it wasn't for him.  That's

why I said that little Jeremi child, Honey, she'd have

to go.  I will tear a bitch up if they get within ten

feet of my Boo.  I'll give them five seconds to back

off and then, Bitch, I'ma wreck shop!"  We both burst

into laughter at the thought of it.

# I'm On My Own

Once we reached my new apartment everybody jumped out and grabbed some things to carry, and up to the second floor of the building we went. The building was pretty quiet, with three floors and an apartment located on each. The halls and stairways were very clean; I was really happy that it looked exactly as it did when the landlord showed us the place. With the way my day had started, I was in no mood for a bait and switch. When we got all my boxes and stuff loaded into the apartment, Mama J and I prepared lunch for everyone, we had stopped at the grocery store on the way in which was only about ten minutes away. It was such a nice feeling to look around and see everybody gathered in my livingroom and chilling out. I felt like a grown up for once, like I was in control of my steps and I could either succeed or screw up, I was really happy. Uncle Joe was sitting on the couch talking to Papa J and Whalid about some sports scores,

when Jay-Jay walked by coming back from the bathroom,
he grabbed him by the arm and said, "What's been up
Lil' Jay?" Jay-Jay just smiled and said, "I'm alright
Uncle Joe." Uncle Joe gave Jay-Jay a strange look and
said, "You are still a little uncomfortable around me
aren't you? I told you, I love you Jay, you can let
your guard down, when Uncle Joe's around, it's all
good Baby." Papa J jumped in, "I noticed that to Jay-
Jay, we are all family; true family, we don't play
games, we love you." Uncle Joe then grabbed Jay-Jay
by the waist and sat him down on his leg and said,
"From the first time we met, I told you; I'm a man and
I have no questions about my manhood, and no problems
with yours. Do you Nephew, and don't worry about
other folks and what they think. If I hug you or sit
you on my lap, it is as an uncle; you understand that,
and I understand that and we don't need to explain the
shit to anyone else, do you understand? Do you see
what I mean, you should be totally comfortable sitting
on my leg just like T is, it's all family Baby. And
that's just who y'all are to me, I don't hug Wade or
Whalid and I wouldn't dare sit neither one of the
niggas on my lap, 'cause that's not who we are to each

other.  But when it comes to you and Topaz it's just like dealing with my own child, there's nothing shady or unnatural about it, now gimme some love!"  He grabbed Jay-Jay in a tight bear hug and kissed him on the forehead and said, "Uncle Joe loves you Man."  Jay-Jay got up from his leg and said, "I do understand and I love you guys too!"  I smiled at Jay-Jay's eyes filling with tears.

By 8pm folks started stirring and getting ready to get moving to go home; we made jokes that maybe Jay-Jay should drive back because it was well past Mama and Papa J's bedtime.  As we walked down the stairs and out of the building we past an amazingly beautiful female, she stopped and said, "Hello everyone, you must be my upstairs neighbors."  I said, "No; just me, how are you?"  She responded, "Hello gorgeous, my name is Akai and you are one of the most beautiful people I have ever seen."  I smiled and said, "I was just thinking the same thing about you; my name is Topaz.  It's a pleasure Akai."  We hugged and I said, "We will definitely see more of each other, these are my family members and I'm sure you will see them again as well."  She smiled and said,

"I'll catch up with you later Sexy." She continued to make her way into her first floor apartment as we continued outside. I hugged everyone and told them thank you for moving me in as they all piled into the car. Jay-Jay sat in back with Uncle Joe and said, "I'ma call you later, cause you need to look out for Miss Thing on the first floor; she's gonna try to turn you, ha-ha." I said, "Shut up Jay-Jay!" Mama J laughed and said, "I was thinking the same thing Jay-Jay; be careful Baby." Uncle Joe said, "Y'all clownin' if I were twenty years younger y'all wouldn't have to worry about it, 'cause I'd roll up here on the weekends and I would handle that lil' tenderoni." As they continued clowning around I noticed that Whalid had not gone near his truck, I thought to myself, 'What now?' Papa J pulled away from the curb and off they went, I turned to Whalid and said, "Thanks for everything Whalid." He replied, "No problem Boo-Bear, you know I'll do anything for you." I started back toward the apartment building, as Whalid began following me he said, "I wanna holler at you for a minute Luv." I continued walking forward and rolled my eyes up in my head. This was the last thing that I wanted to happen, I couldn't imagine that anything he had to say would be of interest to me.

Once back inside my apartment I climbed onto the couch and sat in an Indian stance with my feet underneath me. Whalid came over and sat right beside me, so close that I could smell the piece of peppermint candy that he was sucking on. I tilted my head to the right and gave him a look, he said, "What; don't be like that T!" I said, "Don't be like what Whalid? You're trippin' and acting like we're all good. We're okay and cordial but all this bullshit right here… No-no." He sat still and looked at me as if he couldn't believe what I was saying. I said, "Excuse me, can you move. I don't want you this close, I'm serious." He slid over to the edge of the couch and said, "Have it your way, but I know better, you are really trying to stay mad, but I am not going to give up on us." I interrupted, "Us; there is no us Boy!" He said, "Don't start getting all loud, you still got feelings for me, admit it. You're still wearing your ring and that says you still love your man!" I stood up and said, "Are you really that stupid? Me wearing my ring has nothing to do with you; it was a gift to me that symbolized something special in my life." He said, "Your right, Me! That ring is my commitment to you, I will always love you T, and I have told you that a million times." I interrupted, "That may be the case with you, but you have no commitment or attachment to me, you broke all of that down – I don't trust you and I don't need you in my life. You are a cheater, and a liar and you have a mean spirit. I don't need any of that in my world! I wear my ring because it is topaz and my name is Topaz and it looks good on me, it has nothing to do with you, at all." Whalid remained quiet as he rose to his feet and stood in front of me and remained quiet, he had a very intense look in his eyes. I didn't know what to think, so I just stood my ground and acted unbothered. He then said, "Look at you, I still make you nervous; that's because you're mine, don't you know that." He grabbed me around my waist and pulled me up close to him so tightly that I could feel his heart beating and his manly parts throbbing. I immediately became uncomfortable, because I knew that deep down, what Whalid was saying was true. I was as mad as hell at him, but I still cared for him,

and being in that close proximity was driving me wild.
How I longed for his caress and that long-lasting
lovers' stroke that drove my body into ecstasy
everytime we connected. I could feel myself drifting
into his clutches yet again, as I told myself, 'No
way.' I tried to mumble the words but they would not
escape my lips. Within the next moments I had been
hoisted into the air and carried into the bathroom.
Not long after reaching the bathroom all of our
clothes were off. Whalid got into the tub and laid
stretched out the full length of the vessel, he then
told me, "C'mon bring your sexy ass on in here," he
then lowered my body on top of his and turned the
water from the shower head full blast. I was so
turned on as the steaming hot waters' force beat me on
my back and trickled down my sides and onto Whalid's
beautiful chocolate skin. It was as if our bodies
were morphing into one another. Although the tub was
tight with the both of us in there, I felt amazingly
safe in his grasp, just the way I used to. I laid my
head against his shoulder and relaxed as his hands
rapidly caressed my every nook and cranny. Before
long we were absolutely slippery with the running

water and the liquid soap. As we lay surrounded in the steam that was filled with the scent of botanical gardens, I felt like I was in heaven. After about twenty minutes I could tell this ferocious foreplay was causing Whalid to want to burst, he motioned for me to stand up and rose to his feet to join me; he picked me up and placed my back against the beautifully tiled wall with one hand while venturing inside my body with a few fingers of the other hand. All of a sudden my mind took a path of it's own; as he maneuvered in my region with his hand I could feel my back sticking to the wall which set off a terrible déjà vu within me. My mind was almost immediately wisked away to the first sexual encounter that Tylique and I shared; he had placed me on the shower wall in this same manner. I felt my heart drop as a ball of confusion set in; at that moment I was longing for Tylique. How I would love to be at the mercy of his shower wall attack. I returned to my present state of mind and affairs and told Whalid, "Please put me down." He stopped what he was doing and said, "Huh, what's the matter?" I said, "I can't do this, please let me out." He replied, "T, don't do this, talk to me, what's wrong?" I pulled away from his grip and said, "I can't do this with you, and I'm sorry I even let this get started this, this is stupid, and I - I just can't." I jumped out of the tub and stormed out of the bathroom, wetting the floor as I walked across the hallway and into my bedroom. I grabbed a towel out of one of the opened boxes on the floor, I wrapped my bottom half with it. Seconds later Whalid followed me into the room and I could feel the tension in his every step, he grabbed me by my arms and said, "What the hell are you trying to do T? What little game are you playing now?" I responded, "I promise you I am not playing any games, I am just being real with the situation at hand. This is not gonna work, it's just gonna make things worse." He yelled, "Bullshit, I want you and you want me. The whole time we were in that tub your dick was hard, and dicks don't lie; not even on a nigga that don't even use his. Your body wanted me inside; you can't deny it. Why don't you stop this bullshit and finish what you started." I said, "What I started; how did I start it. Did I pick you up? Did I carry your big ass anywhere? I didn't start this shit Whalid Jesper!" He grabbed a towel out of the box and said, "I could really choke your ass right now!" I said, "There he is, I was wondering when the real Whalid was going to show up." He just gave me a dirty look; I said, "Again, thank you for helping me, and good night, we are done here."

Silence fell over the room as Whalid stomped around retrieving his clothing, his anger and frustration was evident. I just kind of watched him as he beautiful body passed back and forth, I actually felt bad that this was happening. I could tell that he was hurt and that's where the anger was coming from. All that said; I understand his feelings, but I can't allow myself to go back down that road, too much had gone on, too much hurt had been placed in my lap and I really was not over it and I don't know if I ever will be.

Once he had everything on he stormed down the hallway toward the livingroom, he picked up his glass of soda that he had left on the table and drank the remainder of what was in the glass in one gulp. He turned to me and said, "So this is it; this is how you really wanna leave this shit T?" I said, "I'm sorry Whalid, I have to; I'm not trying to…" he cut my

statement with the deep clearing of his throat.  He
then proceeded to walk into my kitchen, I followed him
as I thought to myself, 'Why are we dragging this out,
just leave.'  He stood in the middle of the floor and
said, "How do you form your little dirty mouth to say
that you're sorry and you ain't playin' wit' a nigga's
feelings, but you are standing there with just a towel
on!"  I responded, "Don't start with the dumb stuff!
Whenever you don't get your way then all of a sudden,
everybody's attacking you and then you want to start
insulting folks and acting an ass, grow the fuck up
Whalid!"  He threw his glass into the sink and it
shattered on contact, he then lunged toward me
grabbing me by my arms and yelling, "You got that
smart ass mouth all of a sudden and I ain't diggin' it
at all!  I'm a grown ass man, how's your young ass
goin' be tryna' tell me to grow up, Bitch, I'll slap
the taste right off of your goddamn tongue."  I stood
there and for some reason, there was no fear of any
kind, I just stared him down as he spoke.  And then I
tilted my head a little to the left and said, "You got
two seconds to take your fuckin' hands off of me,
Whalid Jesper!  I am not your child or your property,

so raise the fuck up off of me with your simple ass, that bullying shit is so weak. And calling me bitches, for real! Is that suppose to make me cry, I've cried all the tears that I'm going to cry that concern you. And I've listened to the last of your bullshittin' ass threats, not let's talk real shit…" he had a complete look of shock and confusion on his face as I continued, "Your next move is to clean up that damn glass that you broke like a fuckin' two year old. Then you can roll up outta my house and get in your truck and go back down the road to Christine and Jeremi and God knows who else that ridiculous behavior works for!" He went to say something as I cut him off and raised my hand in front of his face and said, "Shut it!!!!! I don't wanna hear shit else, if you continue, my next move will be the best move of all! Cause quite frankly, I'm growing tired of you and all of your baggage." He grabbed my hand and said, "And what move is that faggot!" As soon as the words escaped his lips I slapped his face as hard as I could. I don't know who was more shocked, me or him.

We were at a stand still for what seemed an eternity, but it was really just a few seconds. I

yelled at him, "How could you call me that! Of all
the things that you have said over this time, you have
never called me that! Are you serious right now!"
Tears began to flood my face as my heart felt as
though it had shattered into a million pieces. He
stood in front of me stoic as if the tears meant
nothing and what he said was acceptable, and then
followed his indiscretion with, "If you ever put your
hands in my face again, I'll knock you the fuck out!"
I responded immediately, "That's really gonna add to
your street cred; that you could knock me out. That
you can get away with calling me out of my name and
treat me like shit. Does that take the sting away?"
He said, "What sting, Bitch!" I said, "The sting that
goes up your spine with the fact that you know that
you are a faggot too!" He mugged me in my face with
on hand hard enough that force made me fall backward
onto the floor and he yelled, "I ain't no faggot;
that's you Bitch!" I got up off the floor and said,
"What makes you different? Cause you're bigger and
louder and like throwing your weight around, nigga
please!" He said, "No, you take dick in your ass!" I
stood back in his face and said, "So if you don't get

fucked then you're not gay; you can kiss as many men as you want, and don't leave out - you can even suck as many dicks as you like; that's ridiculous!  But if that's what helps you sleep at night, then so be it, you clown.  But you should know; that is as dumb as you are!"  I could see the irritation rising in him, but I didn't care, I kept going, I had grown tired of holding all those feelings in.  He said, "Only a fag will let a nigga up on they back!  And you know that you take dick better than everybody I've ever fucked, so that's like you say all the time - it is what it is!"  I could tell from his stance that he felt as though he had secured himself as the argument's victor.  Sorry, not today!  I said, "Let me explain something to you; the only thing that makes you keep revisiting how well I take dick is not the fact that you see me as a fag, it's the fact that you view it as a talent and you can't compete, I really believe that you are just a little jealous.  And also you are correct; to call you a faggot wouldn't be right, that's actually too classy a title to give you, what you are is a Confused-Ass-Common-Cock-Sucker and I'd like you to leave my apartment before I call my dad and my uncle and tell them that the friendly neighborhood pedophile has shown up for a continuation of my ongoing molestation." He began to back away from me and turned toward the door, I said, "And Whalid, before you go, let me ask you…" he turned to face me, I said, "Is the reason that you treat me the way you do now, because I got too old for you?" I chuckled and said, "Ah, nevermind, just get the fuck out Whalid!" He stormed to the door and said, "Let me get the fuck outta here before I really hurt you T!" I stood there and watched as he went out of the door and slammed it, I went over and locked it and said to myself, 'Yet, another win for the fag!!!!!'

## Everything's New

As I lay in my bed I start to really consider that there is something not right about Whalid. It's like he can't stop himself from that strange streak of behavior, as soon as it is outside of his realm of control then up comes this crazed tyrant that does and says whatever is the most hurtful. There is an issue there, just the fact that he could go all this time and never call me a faggot and then just out of the blue, he comes out of his mouth with it and it was said with such malice. I felt no different than when it was said by my family members, I'm sorry but I don't see any type of forgiveness in his future. I'm growing really tired of his bullshit and covering for him, he is the one with the most to lose. But he is so arrogant you would never know it. I'm sure there would be some repercussions with the Jespers finding the full truth, but let's face it, I was a minor and he had most of the control in the situation. All in all I feel that I have dedicated too much of my life to this, it has no validity in my life going forward, and I have said it time after time, but I'm done with this and done with Whalid Jesper.

After what seemed an endless slumber I finally arose at 2:25pm the next day, all that drama had just drained all of my energy. I was thoroughly behind schedule with the things I had planned for the day. I still had to unpack and get everything situated in this apartment, I put on some music and got busy. I was really in my groove while the sounds of Whitney Houston filled the room, I cleaned, unpacked and accompanied Ms. Houston up and down the music scales on every track of the cd. Around 8pm, I heard a knock at the door; I thought, 'Oh boy, I must have my music too loud.' When I looked through the peep hole in my front door I saw the vision of beauty from the first floor. I hurried and opened the door like a kid on Christmas, I said, "Hey Beautiful, how are ya?" Akai stood there in her petite frame wrapped in a pink silky robe, and a warm smile on her face, I could tell that she was equally happy to see me, she said, "What's up Sexy." I said, "Come on in, you have to excuse the place I'm still trying to get it together. Was the music too loud or something?" She replied, "No, not at all, I loves me some Whitney. I came up to see if you'd like to go hang out with me and a few friends in about an hour or so. I told a few of my girlfriends about my sexy-ass neighbor and they are dying to meet you. Please say you'll come!" I stalled for a moment, then I said, "Sure, let me get dressed. What kind of place are we going?" She replied, "To the bowling alley, it's where all the college and folks in their twenties and early thirties hang out on weekends.  So put on something cute; I know you will."  She strutted toward the door as I followed, as she entered the hallway she said, "See ya shortly Gorgeous!"  I smiled and gave a wave as I closed the door.  This should be good, I thought I would be sitting around bored for weeks before I met anyone or learned my way around.  I knew exactly what I wanted to wear, I went to my closet and got it out and laid it on the bed and jumped promptly into a shower.  Within the next 50 minutes I was standing in front of the mirror on the back of my bedroom door examining my get up.  A fresh pair of black True Religion jeans with red stitching details that rested perfectly at my hipline and a red fitted sheer shirt with silver studs on the side and shoulder seams(it was custom made for me by my friend Mike).  I also had a pair of black Jordans with small hints of red on them.  I grabbed my red and black sunglasses off of my dresser and headed for the door.

As I reached the bottom of the hallway staircase the first thing I saw was Akai standing in her doorway smiling, she said, "C'mon in here, we're just having a quick little drink before we leave." As I entered the ultimately girly apartment I was greeted by three really cute and fly females, they were all just as giddy as they could be. I said, "Hello ladies, how are ya?" They were introduced to me one at a time by Akai as she prepared herself a drink. She said, "What do you want to drink Sexy?" I replied, "I don't drink, thanks." "We will change that," and a burst of laughter came from the shortest girl sitting on the couch. Akai said, "I know that's right; Topaz, that is Rebecca. We have been friends since grade school." Rebecca was about 5 foot 4 inches tall with caramel skin and honey-blonde hair styled into a mohawk. She was really sharp and kind of put me in mind of my birth mother. Next was a double vision, sitting on the far end of the couch was a set of identical twins. Very pretty girls with shoulder length hair and quite nice frames, they both stood about 5 foot 8 inches tall. Akai said, "These hoes are my absolute besties, Michelle and Nichelle, we were actually next door neighbors from childhood before we came here to Jackson College." I said, "Oh wow, do you all go to Jackson?" Laughter broke out in the room, I was momentarily confused. Michelle said, "No Topaz, we are all graduates, we work on the campus, when we were attending we could never afford to live over here. Me and my sister have an apartment about ten minutes from here." She then gave me a quick soothing grin as she pushed her crimson red hair over her shoulder. Her and her sister looked so much alike that the only way you could tell them apart is their hair color. Michelle was a dazzling red head and Nichelle's hair was coal black like midnight. Rebecca said, "I also work near the campus at a law firm, I am a legal secretary there, so you'll be seeing plenty of us." I replied, "That's good, I was kind of nervous about not knowing anyone." Akai chimed in, "Don't worry Sexy, I work in the Admissions Office, we will be at your beckon call. I already peeped the fact that you are a spoiled brat, so I plan to keep my eye on you." She winked her eye, I said, "I am not a spoiled brat." She said, "Oh, you are, for what your parents are putting out for you to live here as oppose to living on campus, you're a brat darling. Embrace it, it's cool to have someone love you and genuinely care about your well being." I just smiled, a few seconds later

42

there was a knock at the door, Akai said, "Oh good,
it's Afini." I noticed both twins roll their eyes up
in the heads and Rebecca just chuckled. As Akai
opened the door I got a look at the ugliest girl I
think I have ever seen, she had extremely dark skin,
her joints were a bit ashy and her hair was totally
nappy. Her hair was in a sort of bobbed haircut, but
it had no curls just naps, and dry and brittle. She
was every bit of 300 pounds and only stood about 5
foot 3 inches tall. All of this was topped off with
deep set eyes, dry, cracked lips and a horribly jive
outfit with run over shoes. The funny part was after
speaking to her for a short period you could tell, she
thought she was just as sharp as the rest of the
group, I found it fascinating.

She entered the apartment with robust vigor and a
ghetto stride. "What's up Bitches, I'm ready to get
fucked up tonight!" She stopped as her eyes met mine,
"Who's this?" I said, "Hello, my name is Topaz,
what's yours?" She replied, "That's none of your
concern, Hun." She walked past me and proceeded to
make a drink, then she said, "Akai, what's his point
and tell me he's not going with us." Akai replied,

"He is my neighbor from upstairs and he is coming with us; be nice, he is a very nice guy." Afini said, "He looks ha-ha, NICE," as she motioned her fingers in the air to make air quotes. I could feel myself becoming a little unglued, I was truly not ready to do this right now, I was just trying to push to the side the hurt given just last night with Whalid's comments. Akai said, "Afini, seriously that is so unnecessary, we're trying to have a good time tonight and enjoy new and old friends, no one is trying to be at odds with one another." Michelle chimed in, "Yeah, cut the bullshit, I ain't for it tonight!" Afini didn't back down, she poked her big ugly chest out and said, "Say what y'all want, I don't care for faggots, so I don't have to be nice to him if I don't want to!" The abrupt statement left a silence in the room and eyes were wandering back and forth, but that was it for me, I said, "Hold it, what would make you think that you could just roll up in here talking shit and being all rude. Stating what you like and who you don't need to be nice to. Trust that you got it all fucked up, yes I am gay, but to think that you don't have to be nice to me is incorrect. You will not disrespect me! And as far as me going anywhere with you, huh, that's a joke, I don't even know how you got out of the zoo to get over here today, but you need to get back to your tribe before they realize that one of the gorillas are missing, you Ape-like Bitch!" She stood there in shock, I guess she thought I was just going to take her insult, but much to her surprise she was dealing with the wrong person. I looked at Akai and said, "I'm really sorry for the confusion Akai and the rest of you ladies, I would love to hang out with you all another time, but I don't have this to do." I started toward the door. As Afini said, "Yeah go some where and blow somebody fag!" I turned around and said, "How original was that Magilla-Cuddy, when's the last time someone asked you to blow them, is that why your mad at me. It's bitches like you that make it necessary for folks like me, go get a perm you round motherfucker." I walked out of the door and closed it and went back up to my apartment. I sat on my couch, I was so upset, I really wanted to go out but I'm not dealing with that kind of ridiculous behavior anymore.

Just before I was getting ready to take my clothes off and start back cleaning my apartment there was a knock at my door and when I opened it, there stood the twins, Rebecca and Akai.  Michelle said, "Can we come in Boo?"  I replied, "Of course."  The four of them poured into my apartment, and took a seat on the couch and love seat, Akai started, "We are so sorry about what went down, please don't be upset with us, we had no idea that she was going to do that."  I said, "I'm not upset with you guys, hey, I'm not upset with her ugly ass, I said what I had to say, she is unimportant to my life."  Nichelle said, "Well please still come out with us, we told her to beat it, and we would rather not hang with her tonight.  The funny thing is you have never met her and you said things that I have always wanted to say to her, she can be very negative and aggravating."  I shook my head in disgust and said, "People have their opinions, but they need not voice them out loud in public with the intent to hurt other folks.  But enough about her, aren't we going somewhere."  I locked up my apartment and we were out, we all piled into our cars and drove to the bowling alley which was absolutely packed.

The girls knew just about everyone and they continuously introduced me to folks throughout the night, I thought to myself, 'After the first twenty folks there is no way I will remember anyone else.' It was around 1am when I separated from the girls to go to the restroom, I strolled through the large facility and it was all there.  The stares, the casual smiles, a few chuckles and a few turned up lips, you know the normal – folks don't understand anyone that isn't status quo.  I've grown accustom to the looks. I reached the bathroom and strangely enough I was the only one in there, I went into the stall, took care of my business and as I came out of the stall I was taken totally off guard I just happened to be looking down. Directly in front of me was a pair of Jordans standing facing me; it made me jump a little bit, I didn't hear anyone come in, as my eyes scanned up, my stomach did a flip flop, I was speechless.  "I'm sorry I didn't mean to scare you.  I need to speak to you, is that okay?"  I couldn't move or respond, I just stood there for a moment, then a single tear ran down from my right eye.  Within seconds I was hoisted off my feet and carried back into the stall, as my back was placed against the stall door I could feel my whole body heating up with the need to be swept away.  A kiss that I would never forget took place; all the words that needed to be said were said, and we were on one accord. "T, I missed you so much…" I responded, "I missed you too, Ty." He slid me down his body slowly and said, "I have been watching you since you came in, I am so sorry about everything, I promise I will make it up to you and I will never betray you again. I love you more than I love myself and I will never hurt you again." I replied, "I know." Tylique said, "C'mon let's get up outta here." As we walked toward the door I explained that I hadn't seen him at all, and he made a joke about how true love will turn you into somewhat of a stalker. We opened the bathroom door and to my surprise was Sharif, basically standing guard, I just laughed and said, "Hey Rif, what are you doing here?" He said, "I just came to help my bro settle in and to party a little bit with these lames until school starts. I'm rollin' home on Monday morning when Ty goes to his first class." We spoke a little longer and then decided that the three of us would go to my apartment and continue hanging out when the bowling alley closed. I told them that I would let my girls know, and I would meet them at their car

and they could follow me back home.  As I started back
to the other side of the huge bowling alley Tylique
and Sharif introduced me to three friends of Ty's from
the Philadelphia area, they were really tall and good
looking, I figured they were all there on basketball
scholarships as well.  It was nice to meet them, but
all I could concentrate on was rekindling with my one
true love.  My stomach was doing flip-flops and my
body literally ached for his touch.  Forgiveness was
taking place at a greater rate than I could have ever
imagined.  I was so hurt by the previous acts, but I
knew in my heart and soul it was time to let it go and
move on, and besides, I believed him when he said that
he was sorry and would never do it again.

I explained to Akai what had happened on my trip
to the bathroom, I told her I would explain the rest
to her at another time how I came to be date a
basketball player and she was okay with that, anxious
to know but she'd have to stick it out.  Shortly after
I got back with my crew the alley was closing down, it
was a little after 2am.  We were exiting the doors
into the parking lot and Akai said, "Sexy, this
complex is so huge, we will follow you over to the

other side to make sure you meet up with your dude and
then you can follow us back, just in case you don't
remember the way home, and besides, I wanna get a good
look at this mutha, because if he is nearly as fine as
you I am going to scream!" I chuckled and said, "You
know good and damned well I know how to get home, but
if you'd like to be nosey, have at it, Boo!" As we
dispersed into the parking lot all you heard was the
echo of what sounded like firecrackers going off, and
then chaos, there were folks screaming and scattering.
You also could hear the screeching of what sounded
like a serious get away car. The chaos was coming
from the main entrance way, which is where Ty and
Sharif's crew had parked, you couldn't move your car
at all from the side where we were parked because of
all the cars scattering and trying to get out of the
complex. Myself and the girls decided to be nebby and
go and investigate, as we walked around to the front
of the complex, you could hear a bunch of crying and
screaming for an ambulance, this caused us to speed up
out walking. As we approached the mayhem, I wished
that we had just left the complex with the rest of the
speeding cars. There was deafening screams and cries

and blood all over the ground and a few cars, I could feel my stomach tightening. As I approached I could see two guys stretched out in the parking lot that had been shot, their bodies were absolutely limp and had no life in them what so ever. There was a third guy who was wounded just a few feet away from the two of them, and he was screaming in agonizing pain. There were a few people telling him to hold on and assuring him the paramedics were on the way. As I focused in on the things that the guy was saying, I zeroed in on his Philly accent, my stomach dropped as I took a closer look and I realized these were the three friends that Ty had introduced me to. I was in a panic as I started to explain to Akai, that these were Ty's friends. I needed to know where Sharif and Tylique were in the midst of all of this confusion. The paramedics and the police showed up within the next few moments, they jumped out and immediately assessed the situation and started working on the one guy, the other two were already gone, they covered the bodies as they shooed the people away from the scene. We were so disturbed by everything we hadn't moved, I had never seen such brutal death up close like this, then it hit me that I need to find my folks.  As we walked over about three or four cars there were paramedics and police officers trying to calm a person down and ask questions.  That's when I seen Sharif and Tylique; Sharif just kept saying, "They just shot 'em, Man, they just fuckin' shot 'em!"  He was sitting on the ground and Tylique was lying in his lap with absolutely no movement and the two of them were covered in blood.  I felt my face flush and my legs becoming gummy underneath me and all at once, everything just went black.

# O' Brother

As I regained consciousness my eyes were extremely blurred, I could hardly make anything out, there were just hazy figures and I had no idea where I was. After a few moments I was able to make out who the people in the room were; Akai was sitting at my side holding my hand, the twins were sitting at the foot of the bed and Rebecca was sitting on a chair that was resting at the end of the bed. We were in the emergency room and I had one hell of a headache. Akai said, "Topaz, are you alright? My God, you gave us such a scare," she then turned and said, "Becca grab a nurse please and tell them he's awake." Just then it all came rushing back to me, I sat straight up and said, "Where is Tylique? Where's Sharif?" Then as I looked over to the side I saw Sharif laying in the other bed in our space, he was sedated. Akai held my hand very tightly and said, "Baby, you've got to be real strong for me right now, do you understand? They have sedated Sharif, they didn't want him to hurt himself or anyone else; they did manage to get enough information to contact their parents, and they are on their way." She looked at me deep in my eyes and said, "Topaz, Tylique is gone baby. I'm so sorry." I felt like I was going to throw up, I could feel the tears flooding my face but I couldn't say a word. My head was throbbing and all of the blood curdling details started to flood my memory all the way up to my blackout. After about fifteen minutes of that horrible daze I was in, I felt as though I was gonna be able to handle this. I said, "Why the hell is my head hurting so bad?" By this time the nurse and Rebecca were stepping into the area and the nurse said, "You hit your head on the ground pretty good young man." I could feel the knot that had formed on the side of my head. She then asked the girls to leave the room, I said, "No please, let them stay, I don't know what would've happened to me if they hadn't been there." She replied, "That's fine." She then proceeded to check out my vitals and then a policeman came in to question me on what I saw at the bowling alley. The girls had already been questioned, and they were doing okay, they were a bit shook up, but they were okay.

I looked at the time it was almost 5am and I was dreading the fact that Ty and Sharif's parents would be here soon and who knows how that's gonna go, from what the girls were telling me Sharif was more than a handful. I told them thanks for seeing about me and I told them that I was going to stay with Sharif until their parents came and I would be okay to get home and I would contact them as soon as I knew anything. After a little struggle they agreed to go home, I could tell by looking at them how tired they were.

About fifteen minutes after my crew left, Sharif had started to come around, he was very groggy. I pulled a chair up next to the bed and I started to talk to him. Within moments he was up and around, and shedding tears heavily, he grabbed my hands and said, "They killed him T, for no fuckin' reason, they killed my Baby Bro. I'ma kill me a muthafucka, I promise you that. All we was doing was hanging out, them niggas had some words, we wasn't in that shit. When they started sayin' somethin', me and Ty walked away, then these lil punk-ass bastards goin' spray all of us when we walk out the place, what da fuck T!" I said, "I know Rif, it doesn't make any sense." Sharif looked at me with tears streaming down his face, his long eyelashes drenched and glistening, his grip on my hands got extremely tight as he began to talk at a low volume and an intense pace, "I already considered you family Lil T, now you are the only brother I got left." I replied, "I'm right here Rif, I'm not going anywhere." He briefly cracked an appreciative smile and kissed my hands. We just sat there for the next ten minutes in complete silence, both crying, when all of a sudden I heard a deafening scream unlike anything I have ever heard before. Sharif jumped up and yelled, "Mama!" We ran out of the area we were in and into the open area and sure enough Sharif was right, Mr. Rudolphson was trying to hold his wife up on her feet, she was losing her footing quickly while screaming over and over, "My baby, my baby, they killed my baby!" Mr. Rudolphson was amazingly well composed while dealing with Mrs. Rudolphson, I thought to myself, that is what a man is, I couldn't imagine where he was pulling that inner strength from. Within minutes he had Sharif on the other side of his body and he was holding him up too. It was a scene that I wanted to forget as soon as possible and never experience again, the pain and anguish was just too much, I felt my legs weakening and I just

slid down the wall into a sitting position

while Mr. Rudolphson and some of the staff

tried to gain control of the situation.  One of

the staff members, a Caucasian woman with long

straight blonde hair, said, "Please let's go

over here…" into what seemed to be a conference

room, there were also two homicide policeman

following.  Mr. Rudolphson took Sharif by the

hand and put his other arm around Mrs.

Rudolphson and began to lead them into the

room.  As they got to the doorway I heard him

say, "Are you people for real; I have my wife

in one arm and my son in the other and you lead

me into a room and leave my other son sitting

on the floor in the hallway!  If someone

doesn't carry their ass down that hall and

bring my child to me, there will be another

ugly situation in this god-damned little hick

town tonight!" Everyone stopped in their tracks, and before any moves could be made, Sharif departed from his own grief and said, "I got it Dad, we don't need no one to get him, he's our fam, I'll get him!" Mrs. Rudolphson lifted her head and said, "Yes Sharif, go get Topaz, and bring him to us, he belongs with us." Within seconds Sharif was lifting me to my feet and saying, "I got you, come on Shorty." We returned to the room, took seats at the table and it began again, all of the interrogation.

After about forty-five minutes of the constant questioning I swear Sharif and I were all cried out. It was such a grueling process; to have to keep reliving those events made my stomach turn, I was totally spent. Mr. and Mrs. Rudolphson had to go and identify the body; I couldn't do that, I couldn't stand to

see the love of my life in that state, not one
more time, I just couldn't. Sharif stayed with
me.  He kept telling me over and over how much
it meant to him that I had stayed by his side
through all of this.  He also held on to a
slight cryptic look when he swore to avenge
Ty's death.  I said, "And what am I suppose to
do if you go to jail Rif?  I know you're mad, I
am too, but I can't risk losing both of you to
the same assholes and their bullshit.  But I
know it hurts, they still have not found the
fools that killed my brother and his father,
and it seems as though they just flat out,
stopped looking, it is disgusting.  But what
can you do?"  Sharif looked at me again with
his long, dark, wet eyelashes glistening and
said, "You are speaking all truth to me Shorty
and I love you for it, but I'm as mad as hell!"
I could see his thuggish side becoming very

prominent, it was almost scary. I grabbed his hand which was cold and still, and I said, "I know Rif, but just take your time, don't rush into anything," I paused and then continued as his hand warmed up and he held onto my hand and the rough edge dissipated, "Use your head, you're older than me and Ty, so I know I can't tell you what to do, but just make sure you don't ruin your life trying to avenge Ty's. He would not want that, and you know that." We just sat in silence until his parents came back for us. Mr. Rudolphson came up and said, "Okay fellas, it's time to go." Sharif and I stood up and the four of us headed toward the exit doors of the hospital. It felt as though we were moving in slow motion and I had an eerie feeling that I was forgetting something. The closer I got to the door the more my anxiety built, we stepped outside of the doors and the sunlight blasted us, it felt as though we had just emerged from a cave. We all just stood still for a moment like we were all thinking the same thing and the next thing that happened shook me to my core.

Mrs. Rudolphson dropped like a boulder, to her knees onto the cement, she stretched her arms forth as though she was on the altar at church and she said, "I can't, God no, I can't!!!!!" Mr. Rudolphson dropped down to console her, but it wasn't working this time, she continued on, "I cannot; I cannot; I cannot leave my baby here! I won't go home without my baby, I won't! I will stay here until that transport him home, but I cannot get in a car and drive two hours away while my baby lays in there. Oh God! Give me the strength!!!!!!" Sharif and I both joined his parents on our knees there in the front of the hospital,

Sharif began to pray, which I have to say, kind of shocked me. Mr. Rudolphson was unsuccessful in gathering his wife, this part of the ordeal was a little over the top for her and she was not having an easy time of it, and strangely enough I totally understood her position. I knew that Mama Jesper would feel the same way about me or Whalid. I then thought to myself, 'What would Mama J have me do in this situation?' And then it came to me, I looked at Mr. Rudolphson and said, "May I?" he gave me a nod, yes, as I seen his eyes for the first time welling up with tears. I took hold of both of Mrs. Rudolphson's hands and I began to sing softly, "When Jesus is my portion, a constant friend is He. For his eye is on the sparrow, and I know he watches me." And with that she lifted her head slowly and our eyes met, she grabbed me in a tight embrace and

said, "My God, my God, my God, my God, my God!"
We all stood and in seconds it seemed we were
gathered, calm and collected. I then said, "I
understand what you are saying and I don't want
him to stay here either, and I know my Mama
would feel the same. When are they going to
send him home?" Mr. Rudolphson replied, "Later
on today, they will transport him to an
undertaker in our town." I said, "It has been
a very long night and morning, my apartment
isn't far from here, why don't you guys just
come over to my place and get some rest, I hate
for you to jump back on the road for those two
hours without resting anyway. And I'm going to
go home as well, but there's no way I could
make that drive right now." Mrs. Rudolphson
said, "I think that's a great idea Topaz, but
we don't want to intrude." I said, "Family
doesn't intrude on one another, you all are my

family and I have felt that way since the day I met you. You are more than welcome to my home." Mr. Rudolphson chimed in, "This will work out, because we don't want you making that drive alone under the circumstances, Sharif has to grab his car too and we can do a caravan back to town, that way we can keep our eyes on all of our boys." He went on, "Topaz, have you contacted your parents?" I replied, "No Sir. I didn't want to upset them, I'll explain everything to them when we are face to face. If I tell them before, they will be too worried." He scolded me a bit and said, "Young man you don't have the authority to decide what we can take and what we can handle. That phone call home is owed to your parents. You have been through a lot, I don't think you even realize it at this point. You were even treated at the hospital, and when we get to your apartment I will call your parents myself;

as parents we owe them that. This situation

could have easily been the other way around and

you could be the one that didn't make it, and

we would want to know about Ty's status, I owe

your parents that, do you understand?" I said,

"Yes Sir, I didn't think of it that way, I'm

sorry." A single tear fell from my eye. He

said, "Oh goodness, don't do that. Ty told me

once he hated it when you would cry, now I see

why." And he and Mrs. Rudolphson both

chuckled, Sharif grabbed me in a bear hug and

said, "It's okay Lil Man."

We went directly to my apartment and as

planned Mr. Rudolphson called my parents and

explained everything and they were appreciative

of the call just as he had said, but a nervous

wreck just as I thought. We all fell asleep

for several hours. Mr. Rudolphson had made the

necessary calls to find out the time that Tylique's body would be transported and we were on the road at the same time in a caravan heading home.  This was definitely not what I had in mind when I thought about my first week away at college.

# The Lesson of Loss

Once I got home I spoke with Mama and Papa J briefly and then went to my room and basically slept for the next twenty-seven hours, with the exceptional text message from Jay-Jay, Sharif and my crew back at the school. During the few times that I was awake Mama J was begging and pleading with me to eat something, but I just couldn't. I sat at the table with her a few times and by the time I tried to eat what was on the plate I was crying and making a mess of the whole situation. Once I got started then she'd get started and then Papa J would have to come and get us both, it was a mess.

Eventually I was able to pull myself together long enough to get myself dressed and try to move forward with the proceedings that were to come. The public viewing of Ty's body was Wednesday and then the funeral the day after; I had no other choice but to put on my game face and push through. I came downstairs and sat in the kitchen by myself for about an hour just going over my surroundings and thinking to myself how lucky I was to be alive, and more so Sharif. He was right there in the line of fire, it was amazing to think how things seem to work out and the decisions that are made completely outside of our control. I came into a place of peace with the whole situation while sitting there at the table, I knew someone had to be left to tell the story(Sharif) and someone that could tell the story of the deeper side of Tylique Rudolphson and how awesome of an individual that he was(me). God doesn't make mistakes when he chooses assignments for people, at least that is what Mama J always tells me and she has never been wrong up to this point. Just as I came out of deep thought I felt my cell phone vibrating in my pocket, I pulled it out and glanced at it, the screen read, 'Sharif' I immediately answered, "Hey Rif, wassup?" He responded, "Hey Lil Dude, are you finally up; you been sleepin' yo' ass off." I chuckled a bit and said, "The truth of the matter is, I couldn't stand being woke, but I'm good – what about you Rif, how are you feeling?" He got quiet for a second then said, "Man, I feel like I'm gonna lose it. I been spinnin' and the only person I wanted to talk to was you." I said, "Where are you now Sharif?" He replied, "At the top of your street." It kind of startled me, but I said, "I'll meet you at the front door Rif." I hung up my cell and proceeded to the front of the house, the house was quiet and empty, I figured this is good because he will be comfortable with it just being us. He'll be able to say whatever he feels and I hope it will help to bring him out of this dark corner that he is occupying.

A few seconds later as I approached the door I see a silhouette at the door that looked reminiscent of a horror movie. When I slide the blinds and look out of the glass I see Sharif with his hair literally standing all over his head, he just looked flat out - hood and scary. I opened the door and we kind of just stood and gave each other a good look over, Sharif's eyes were as empty as that fashion statement he was making. In one swift movement he grabbed me in an embrace that actually had my feet dangling over top of his; he carried me into the house and used his foot to close the door, all the while never letting me out of his embrace. I just went along with it, I felt so bad for him, he did appear to be lost somewhere in this extreme grief. He finally let me down and said, "Wow, Lil Dude, I needed that!" Tears were just steadily streaming down his face, I could see the thug persona slowly fading and the softer, more calm Sharif was returning. I said, "Come with me, are you hungry?" He responded, "Nah, not really." So I lead him to the stairs and we descended down into the game room. I turned on the television and took a seat on the couch and said, "Tell me what's going on Rif." He sat with his legs parted, feet planted flat on the floor as he kept nervously messing in this mound of hair piled in a crazy formation on the top of his head. Then he began to speak, "I been just driving around for the past two days, at one point I was so mad I really felt like I was losing my mind, I really want to kill somebody. Them three dudes gotta go Shorty; I'm telling you, they gotta go. If Ty can't breathe, why should they? I drove back down to Jackson last night and rode all around that bitch just hoping to see one of dem niggas, I had my strap, I was really goin' pop em' but I found out that the cops had picked all three of them up and they were in custody. I ran into a couple of the dudes from Ty's dorm who recognized me, they're the ones that told me that the three dudes had been taken into custody. I guess that little bit of information settled my anger for a while, I came back to town and I have really just been riding around." I said, "What about your parents Rif? How are they doing?" Quiet permeated the room as Sharif lowered his head and stared at the floor. I broke the silence by grabbing a handful of the hair that he had standing on top of his head and turning his head gently toward me; he cracked a slight smile and said, "What?" I replied, "What, nothing, I know you are not telling me that you have not seen nor spoken to your parents. Sharif that's crazy, I know they have got to be worried sick about you, you have got to call them." As we were speaking I could hear my parents entering the house, I said, "Come on and let me get you together Rif, this has got to stop, I'm good right now and I want you to be good too. First thing's first, that hair is damn scary, I started to run from you. Where is one of those thousands of girls that usually braids this mess, can't you call one of them?" He said, "Nah Shorty, I can't be bothered wit' all dat right now, can't you do it?" I replied, "I ain't no damn hairdresser, Boy!" He laughed and said, "Oh so since I ain't chasin' you down and tryin' to be in love witchu, you can't hook me up?" I said, "Who do you know that chased me anywhere and that's not it at all, besides I do know how to braid, but I don't like it." I sat there and he dropped his big head into my lap and laid there staring up at me like a spoiled child, with his eyes glistening, resting behind those most gorgeous, black eyelashes. Those eyelashes somehow seemed to be the watchmen to his very soul; I was going to have to figure their secret code because I wasn't going to make a life of being held captive and to his beacon call. I ran upstairs and greeted my parents at the kitchen, I told them Sharif was over and not feeling too good. They were concerned as well, I hollered for him to come up and a first glance Mama J moved so swiftly across the kitchen it was startling. She grabbed him in a embrace and said, "This is not it Baby, this is not how you are going to go through this, we got enough love to go around, I feel like you are one of my children, as was Tylique. Topaz, take Sharif upstairs and grab him some of Whalid's things and help him get himself together. We are going to have some dinner and try to get on track with what everyone is in need of to get through this time. We want to be of help. How are you folks Sharif, how are they holding up?" I interrupted, "He hasn't been home and hasn't seen them." Papa J chimed in, "NO, NO, NO. We will call them, they are probably crazed wondering what's going on with you. Go with T,

Trudy and I are going to call your parents.  Go on, off with the two of you."

I led Sharif upstairs and into Whalid's room, I showed him to the bathroom in Whalid's room and gave him a towel and wash cloth, he immediately started stripping down.  I said, "Slow down partner, let me go."  He laughed and said, "What you worried about, I ain't got nothin' you never seen before."  I kept it moving out of there as I caught an unwanted glance of his wrestler's physique.  I grabbed a pair of sweats and a t-shirt from Whalid's drawer, I then sat on the edge of the bed and started texting back and forth with Jay-Jay.  Before long I heard the water shut off, and moments after that, in the same fashion that his brother did it, Sharif walked right out into the bedroom area with the towel drying his hair and stark naked on the bottom.  I couldn't help but stare, for whatever reason I could not take my eyes off of him. His body was chiseled in every spot possible; clothes absolutely did this boy no justice.  He had just enough body hair in all the right places and it looked like you could bounce a quarter off of him at any angle.  I handed him the clothes and watched as he put them on, I knew he had to notice me staring but I couldn't have cared less. Once he finished getting into the clothes he said, "So are you gonna hook me up or what Shorty?" As he threw his towel on my head and laughed as he picked me up and slammed me onto the bed. He lifted me just like a feather, it was effortless. I could feel butterflies in my stomach as he mounted me and straddled my body like the Wolfman lowering himself onto a piece of his prey. He shook his half wet, shoulder length hair in my face while laughing hysterically, he then rubbed his hair onto my stomach, I laughed and said, "Boy, you are getting me all wet with your foolishness. Let me up." He said, "Not till you promise to braid my hair." I replied, "I will, but you need to get up, and let me up, now." Sharif had a puzzled look on his face, he said, "Did I hurt you, I'm sorry Lil' Man, I forgot you are delicate and I can't just toss you around like I used to do Ty." I laughed and said, "Don't be funny; I'm not delicate, punk." He smiled and said, "Yeah you are, I probably broke something, that's why you wanna get up." I said, "Okay, smart ass, I'm not hurt, you didn't break anything, I'm uncomfortable, because I

can feel your thing on my stomach. Since you just had
to know." He rose up and grab a handful of himself
and said, "Don't try to act like you scared of that, I
already know from Ty that you know how to keep that
under control, and just in case you didn't know, my
dad hooked us both up." He grabbed hold with the
other hand as well and said, "Yeah buddy!" I pushed
him off of me and said, "Cut out your crap and let's
get this over with, fool."

I sat on the edge of the bed while Rif sat on the
floor between my legs as I did 'the World's fastest'
set of corn rolls. The whole time my mind was
wandering into dark corners that it had NO
BUSINESS!!!!!

Actually it was a bit nerve-wracking; my flesh
was crawling with the thought of Sharif having his way
with me. Would it be better than Tylique? Hell I had
now seen them both naked and I was impressed on both
accounts. Why is my mind toying with this, this is so
wrong. I am walking around harboring secrets about
Whalid and I truly don't need anymore drama, and as I
said, this right here is just flat out wrong. On top
of the fact, Sharif is straight, he doesn't have any

interest in being gay or indulging in a homosexual act. Does he?

We went down to the kitchen and had dinner with my parents and the conversation started light but quickly went deep. Deep into Sharif's thoughts and emotions on the loss of his baby brother. He was definitely angry and had never really given thought to the fact that he was lucky to be alive, actually he felt a little guilty. He shared that it would've been easier had it been him, he went on to explain that he hasn't really done anything since graduating high school, he hasn't had a job or done the right thing, he said he had been a low profile hustler. Dealing a little drugs here and there, just enough to keep himself some pocket change. He said it didn't take his mom and dad long to figure it out and they do not approve and are always on him to either straighten up or leave home. They said they do not want that type of drama around them or their home, but they have not had the strength to kick him out. By the time he got all of that off of his chest he was just in tears, it was really sad to watch, and being the cry-baby I am, you know my face was leaking too. Papa J got up from his seat and took Sharif into the livingroom and left Mama J and I in the diningroom. Mama J said, "There's a need for some serious man to man talk, right now. This whole situation can be a turning point in Sharif's life - for good or for bad. I hope Wade can reach him, he has such a good spirit, but he is throwing himself into a life that he doesn't belong in at all. I can see in the way that he deals with you that he has a softer, very caring side. I truly believe he is sincere in wanting to know that you are alright with this situation - I hope that is what I'm reading, or do we have to have another type of conversation, my son?" I looked straight ahead at Mama J and didn't say one word, I just thought to myself, 'How the hell does she do that!' She cleared her throat and said, "Topaz Jesper, I am speaking to you and I am expecting an answer, so let's have it." I replied, "What are you talking about Mama J?" Her right eyebrow raised up and she said, "Okay then, here we go, guilty as charged. Let me give you a bit of advice, if Ty was here, would you date his brother? No you wouldn't, so don't use this as an excuse to do something that you normally wouldn't - it's not a good look, at all!" I just sat there with a knot in my stomach. She continued, "You two are young, and you are confusing the bond for something else. And it's not just you; it is Sharif too." I interrupted her, "Mama we haven't done anything, and Sharif is straight. I can't lie, I do find him attractive and I don't know why. It's only been a few days and for some reason it's like someone turned a light on him, before all this I didn't pay Sharif any attention. But now I'm afraid because if you can see that something is there, he probably can too and I don't want to offend him. Oh gosh, I am so embarrassed." She stood up and said, "Boy, help me to clear these dishes. And for the record, I'm sure he has caught on and he is sniffing." I had a puzzled look on my face, she continued, "Though Sharif may actually be straight; Baby, that man is sniffing around you, he is probably as confused as you are. You two share a tragedy that is drawing you two together emotionally. Literally you are the only two who knows how the other feels. You both loved Tylique and you both shared the horrid event that ended his life. Emotions are high and certain lines have become blurred, and trust me that line of straight versus not straight is just about non-existent right now – do not ruin the friendship and the brotherhood over something that is not genuine or going to last.  You will be setting yourself up to be hurt and trust me most of the hurt is going to fall into your lap, listen to your momma Topaz.  This is where you gain a friend and a brother, not a mate."  I looked up at Mama J and smiled, I knew deep down she was dead on, as usual.  She could always read me like a book, it was actually kind of scary at times.

Around 9:20pm Papa J and Sharif emerged from the livingroom and it seemed that everything had gone well; by this time Mama J had gone to bed.  Papa J said, "Alright fellas I'm gonna head off to bed, the old lady has already left me.  And Sharif, just remember what we talked about it's all gonna work out.  And you two continue to have each other's back, it's gonna be a tremendous help to you in the next few days."  We both nodded yes as Papa J disappeared up the stairs.  I grabbed Sharif by the hand and led him down the stairs to the gameroom.  He sat on the couch and I got up on the couch and sat in an Indian stance with my legs folded underneath me. I said, "So do you want to talk or are you all talked out." He replied, "Not really, I'm cool. What do you want to talk about?" I was nervous but I had to know, so I blurted out, "Do you know why me and Ty broke up?" He didn't even hesitate to answer; he said, "Nah Shorty, he just said, 'Rif man, I fucked up, then there was a lot of cryin' and he wouldn't talk for awhile. He was fucked up about you. So I figured that he cheated on you and got caught, am I right?" I replied, "For the most part. But it's cool, I forgave him, he was the love of my life, and I figured that out shortly before I ran into the two of you at the bowling alley and it seems that he and I were thinking the same thing. I'm gonna count it as a blessing that we got to squash it and he knew that I loved him." I was fighting my tears and losing, Sharif grabbed my face and said, "It's cool to cry Shorty, he loved you too. He would tell me all the time, I didn't understand how he could be in love with another dude. But who cares, he was happy. After being around you though, you don't remind me of another nigga, you are just like being with a broad, it's crazy. I have to constantly remind myself that you're a dude." He started laughing, but I wasn't all that amused, I said, "Whatever Rif, you're a clown." He said, "Awww, don't get mad. You're soft and squishy, but that works for you. And Ty said the booty is off the hook!" I punched him in the arm and said, "Hey, shut up, y'all shouldn't have been talking about me like that." He said, "Why not, that was my baby bro, we talked about everything, and I do mean everything. I know what you did and when you did it, and what position you were in, it's no big deal. He had no complaints." I said, "Oh gosh, it's just weird that's all. Those are not things that you should know about me, it's a little embarrassing. Like when you are laughing at me sometimes, I don't know what you're laughing about, that's weird Rif. It kind of gives you the upper hand on me." He started doing the exact laugh that I was talking about, and I punched him in the chest and turned my back to him. He continued laughing and said, "Come on Shorty don't get mad, it's just funny is all. All the stuff my lil bro said about you is all true and it's funny to see you acting it out in person. I laugh cause it's funny to see a lil dude be so emotional and dramatic like a chick.  You are just as moody and dramatic as any broad I've ever boned.  And I think I…" he suddenly became silent.  After a minute I turned around and looked at him sitting there looking like the cat had run off with his tongue.  And I pounced on the open opportunity to take control of this conversation, I said, "And you think you what mouth-a-matic?  What were you gonna say, what was getting ready to come out of that trap of yours that cut off your comedy show you had going."  He just looked at me and smiled and said, "I wasn't getting' ready to say nothin', nothin' at all."  I rose up onto both my knees on the couch and leaned into his face and said, "I think you are lying, and you're not very good at it Sharif Rudolphson."  He said, "You think you know everything don't you?" his mood was still jovial so I continued with my pursuit for the truth.  I said, "I think you like the fact that I remind you of a girl, why do you think that is so interesting Rif?"  All of a sudden we were sitting in silence staring at each other, after a few moments I thought to myself, 'Oh gosh, did I go to far?  Is he mad at me now?  Did I just make a mess of this whole situation?'  I slowly started to move away from the close proximity of his face that I was posted in. As I rested comfortably into a sitting position on the couch, I was getting more nervous by the second, because he wasn't saying anything, he was just sitting there like I had shot him with a freezing ray gun from one of those cheap old cartoon episodes. I finally said, "Sharif…" he didn't respond. I said, "Don't do that, don't get all like that on me, if I said something wrong or something that made you uncomfortable, we are close enough for you to tell me and I will apologize, but don't give me the silent treatment." He turned his head toward me and said, "Well you did, you said something that made me uncomfortable." I said, "Well I'm sorry, I didn't mean…" he interrupted me and said, "No apology necessary, you told the truth, I guess you do know everything." I had a puzzled look on my face, and in the moment Sharif stood straight up from his seat on the couch and it was unmistakably evident that everything about Sharif was standing straight up. The butterflies showed up in my stomach as if they were on cue. I was now uncomfortable, I didn't know what to say or do next and I don't think he did either. He said, "You got me questioning myself big time, why is that, why am I having this problem? I've never been attracted to no dudes." I said, "Come on Rif I think I can explain." I got him to sit back down and I said, "Our emotions are running very high because of the present situations that we have been through and the both of us are misconstruing the feelings for sexual ones and they aren't. We are being joined emotionally for the purpose of upholding each other during this time and I believe that is it, nothing more." He listened, but he didn't seem very sold on what I was saying. I said, "What's your feelings on it Rif, what do you think is happening?" He said, "At first I thought I was just trippin' because of all the shit that has gone down, but just then when you leaned in my face and I could smell you, you fuckin' smell like…I don't know, but it hit me and took me in and the next thing I know, my shit was on brick. What the hell, I don't know what that is all about, but it is driving me crazy. This is not the first time it's happened to me when it comes to you. And now I'm embarrassed. Please don't tell anybody, I never had feelings toward any dudes before, it's fuckin' me up,

I don't want to be gay; nothing against anybody that is gay, but I just never seen that for myself. But on the other hand, do you think that is why I had such an easy time accepting Ty being gay – hell, I don't know what to think, this shit got me buggin." I didn't know what to tell him, I definitely sympathized with his overall confusion and I wanted to help, but I didn't really know where to start. He leaned back on the couch and said, "Look Shorty, this shit is still hard as fuck, it's not even tryna go down. I'm concentrating real hard but nothing is working, I'm gonna have to release, damn it. This is fuckin' embarrassing, I'm sorry Lil Dude. I know this is probably uncomfortable for you to, you kinda said you was feelin' me too and I'm all wavin' my shit around you all hard, I'm sorry. I don't know what to do, I'm stuck, I'm horny as fuck and…" I interrupted him, I started laughing, "Now would be a good time to call one of your chicks, don't you think?" He sat up on the edge of the couch and said, "Actually I don't. I keep telling you I ain't feelin' that right now, you seem to be ignoring the things I'm saying to you Shorty. This is about you and I think the only way to satisfy it is with you." I stood up and said, "Sharif, that is not right. I am absolutely in love with your brother, if he were still alive we would not even be having this conversation." He replied, "You are right, but my brother is not here, and though my mind is telling me it is wrong my body is aching to get at you. I been wanting to break you off since the first time I laid eyes on you sitting in our livingroom. I have beat off so many times when you and Ty were in the next room, when he fucks you and I hear you moan it would drive me crazy, and it's a shame but I would even sometimes find myself jealous. The crazy thing is, I've never done any of this and don't even know if I would like it. I've had other gay dudes try to holler at me, I always told them I wasn't with it, and I wasn't, but you fuckin' do somethin' to me and I can't shake it. So what we goin' do Lil' Shorty." I said, "Sharif, this is all kind of weird and even a little stalker-ish, but it is flattering to know that you are attracted to me. Now I have to be honest, I don't know where the feelings I have for you came from, and I don't know how long they will last. Because I don't know what they are based on, and the last thing I want to do is get into something with you and hurt you. And there is also a chance that you will get into it and find out that you aren't really interested in going forward and where does that leave me?" He sat still and quiet, I could tell he was seriously processing what I had said. He said, "Of course, you know you are right, I hate that you are right, you know that don't you, wit' yo lil sexy ass." I said, "At least we got it all out in the open, and we can deal with it. As long as we are honest with each other then it won't get all weird. Do you agree?" He smiled and said, "I gotcha." Immediately after hearing him say that I felt totally at ease with the situation. I was glad the conversation was closing, I was falling fast and my flesh was crying out, I was about ready to throw a blanket or couch cover or something over him, my body was getting so hot sitting there I thought I was going to set the couch on fire, geez. I don't know why I have such a hard time resisting the men in my life, and it seems to be getting more complicated the older I become. And then it seems that every man I fall for turns out to be forbidden fruit, I'm sure there is

some kind of lesson in all this, but what the heck is
it.

Sharif and I sat and watched movies until late in
the night, that boy loves scary movies, I was having a
heck of a time, some of that stuff we were watching
was just gruesome. He just laughed and said, "I ain't
goin' let nothin' get at you Lil' Shorty." I had
started falling asleep around 2 a.m. my head was
drifting forward, Sharif took and laid me back against
his chest, I said, "Rif, no, it's not the right time
for this." He said, "Hush, and lay back, you got a
blanket around you, I got a blanket over me and you
snorin' so really how sexy is this. Just relax,
nothing is gonna happen that you don't want to happen,
I wouldn't do that." I said, "Ty told me how you
could always talk the chicks into anything." He
smiled and said, "He ain't lie to you, I can talk them
broads out they drawls. But I ain't tryna do that to
you, if I was I wouldn't have been sitting here
earlier with a hard on for an hour and a half, I
woulda figured out a way to get it into your hands or
your…" I interrupted him, "That's enough Rico Suave, I
get the idea. It's nice that you think I'm as weak as

those scrubs you been sexing, and for the record, I don't snore, punk." He grabbed my head and pulled it in to his chest and said, "Okay, take yo ass back to sleep." I did just that, I laid into him and grabbed some of the best rest that I've had in awhile, I felt absolutely whisked away. I knew that I was entering a dangerous place, but I kept telling myself, 'I got this; this is a far as it goes!'

I woke up when I heard Mama and Papa J stirring around and getting ready for work. Sharif was sleeping like a baby and holding on to me like a life raft, I just laid there while repeatedly telling myself, 'I'm in control.' I shifted my body slightly and everything became oh too real, the small movement I made kind of, how can I say it, unleashed the beast. I just laid really still with hopes that he wouldn't wake up and it would just go back down. I could feel the constant throbbing through the covers on my lower back, it was driving me crazy and literally about to set my soul afire. Just as I thought I couldn't stand under the pressure any longer, I heard my parents going across the first floor toward the kitchen and a few seconds later they proceeded to the front door.

For some reason, them being so close, but not really that close, put my fire right out, but it didn't do much for Sharif. At least one of us was under control, at least momentarily.

What I was finding is that Sharif wasn't playing the game totally by the rules, he was awake the whole time when I was struggling not to wake him. So I said to myself, 'Are you gonna try to really play this game like this Rif, I got you!' I warned him that I wasn't one of those little chicks that fall for his crap. I went right along with him and followed his lead, I acted just like I was back asleep. He continued on playing some really dirty tricks for about the next fifty minutes. He caressed his face against mine; tightened and loosened his grip on me; he wrapped his legs around me and even got bold enough to start slightly pumping me. I have to admit, that pumping and leg wrapping almost made me lose it, but I held on. And as a last cheap shot he literally licked the outside of my ear, I gave him no response. He finally stopped and I thought, 'Okay, my turn.' I unwrapped my blanket and turned over and found myself a comfortable spot and laid out on the front of his body and laid my head ever so lightly on his chest and went into a slumber that ultimately drove him over the edge. He was having a really hard time faking sleep with me just about facing him, I could feel his heart rate speed up and from the waist down there was a throbbing that was deeper, faster and harder than his heartbeat itself. I knew I had won when he literally gave up the fake sleep act and shoved his hands under the blanket and into my pants, gripped my cheeks and began to grind into me with such force that I could hardly catch my breath, it seems he forgot his plan and the subtle game he was playing was out of the window and he was moving in for the kill. He was moaning and groaning in such a manner that I was totally captivated, it was so animalistic, like nothing I had ever experienced. I couldn't take anymore, I was losing myself and all control of this situation, I broke free from his grip and leaped to my feet. I said, "Sharif, what was that?" He said, "Proof that you want me as much as I want you." I said, "Fine, I admit it, but it doesn't make it right, and the bottom line is, I would love to go through with this thing, I think it would be extraordinary for

both of us, but then what. Where does it leave me -
Is this a one time thing or are you gonna continually
sneak around and lay up with me, I don't wanna be your
dirty little secret. You have a list of chicks, I
don't want to be the one novelty fuck on the list
either. Plus the fact that you and Ty are brothers
makes me seem a bit whorish, don't you think. I'm
sorry Rif, I have never slept with anyone that wasn't
at least promising an ongoing relationship. Do you
understand, please say you do, because I know you are
not prepared to offer that." He said, "I get it, it
makes me sad, but I do understand. Man, shit I was
ready to split you in two." I said, "I'll make a deal
with you," he was all ears, I continued, "You hold on
to the curiosity, don't go looking for other boys to
split and I will give some real thought to having a
one time all out episode with you, we do it once and
walk away and never talk about it or revisit it
again." Of course he nodded his head in agreement. I
said, "I'm going to take a shower, you overheated me
with all that craziness, I need to cool off." He
replied, "I'm hot too, can I come." I said,
"Certainly, you go to Whalid's shower, and I'll go to

mine and then I'll meet you in my room, and we can
watch some tv or something." He laughed and said,
"Damn, that's a definite cool off." I smiled and up
the steps we went.

After I got out of the shower I went straight to
my room, Sharif still hadn't come out of Whalid's
room. When I finished drying off and lotioning my
body I felt so refreshed, I laid across my bed with
just my towel wrapped around my bottom half trying to
decide what I wanted to put on. Shortly after here
comes naked Sharif, he walks into the frame of my
bedroom door and stands striking some bodybuilding
pose. I said, "You never stop trying do you, with
your corny ass." He said, "Are you saying you don't
like looking at this, come on, don't lie. Cause I
ain't goin' lie, I'm getting horny looking at you in
that towel, this shit is crazy, I don't know what's
wrong with me, your mom must've put something in that
food last night." I said, "Whatever, trust me, my
mother would not approve of me and you hooking up, at
all." I then took my towel off and rolled my naked
body onto my stomach and said, "So I guess we are
going to have a secret between us…" He stood there in

the door like a goon, and after a few moments he said, "Oh shit, you mean right now!" I said, "Right now, hurry up before I change my mind." He leapt across the room like a panther and pounced on me and started working it out like he was never going to get it again, he took such care and pride in every touch. He asked me for a condom, I asked him, why he didn't have one and he replied, "I didn't come here for this but please don't tell me you don't have one, cause if you don't I'm gonna cry." I sent him over to the top drawer in my dresser to grab one and on his way back I took in a look at him and thought to myself, 'Damn, if I'm gonna keep a secret, give myself away and act out of character at least he is worth it.' I sat up on the bed and I looked him in his eyes as we made that most intimate connection and I said to him, "Remember, this didn't happen and can never happen again." He replied as the puzzle pieces fit snug and complete into their destination and his head and eyes rolled back, "Uh, okay - mmm hmmm!" I thought, 'Oh shit, what have I done!!!!!'

We rocked and rolled all over my room for a complete four hours off and on. We made use of the bed, the floor, the dresser, the door and the chair. It was better than I imagined it would be, and Sharif felt the same, he didn't even have to voice it. Every time we made a connection a small tear would run out of his left eye and as his body jerked when breaking the connection multiple tears showed up, he kept trying to hide them. I thought it was cute. As we ended our episode, we just laid and watched television for about thirty minutes, then he said, "I gotta go, so I can be ready for all of this craziness tonite. I know this is a one time thing but it was like going to heaven, thank you LT." He leaned down to kiss me, I turned my head away and said, "LT, what's that?" He said, "Duh Lil' Topaz!" He proceeded with his kiss, a kiss that was meant for me to never forget, a kiss that literally left a signature that stated, 'Good Luck on wiping me from your memory!'

In all of the forbidden satisfaction that had taken place this afternoon, I just hope that I haven't damaged my friendship. I immediately regretted the decision to go through with this episode as soon as Sharif walked off of the porch, I don't think I could stand another loss; not so soon.

**<u>Rest In Peace</u>**

It seems as though the time flew by after Sharif left my house, and before I knew it I was dressed and leaving home for O'Tooles Funeral Home for the public viewing of Tylique. I was really not feeling fashionable or confident, for the first time in a very long time, I didn't even care what I looked like I just wanted to get this over with. On the way there I was sitting in the back seat of Papa J's car and I was just very quiet my mind was really all over the place, I just couldn't really focus at all. As we approached the street that the funeral home resides on Mama J turned around and said, "Are you okay Topaz?" I replied, "I think so; I guess we will see in a moment." Papa J said, "Be strong son, remember you've got us and the Rudolphsons, we are all here for you. Your brother will be here as well, so you will be surrounded by folks that love you." I didn't even focus on that last piece of that comment; I hadn't seen or spoken to Whalid since our argument. He sent me several text messages that I didn't respond to. I really have nothing to say to him, and especially not about Ty; trust me.

As we walked up to the building I was feeling really anxious, there were a lot of people there, I didn't know them all. I guess a lot of them were the Rudolphson's family and friends. As we entered I did see a few people that were familiar to me from several parties and events that Ty and I had gone to. They were very receptive and they waved hello and one couple actually came up and said, "I'm so sorry, I know Ty was crazy about you, keep your head up." Mama J leaned over and said, "That was very nice of them to say, Ty had some really upstanding friends didn't he." I said, "Yes ma'am, they were always really nice to me." As we reached the doorway to the room the Ty was in, the first thing I saw was Mr. and Mrs. Rudolphson standing next to the doorway and Sharif sitting in a chair off to the side. My parents greeted them with hugs and Mrs. Rudolphson told my parents, "We know this has been hard on your family as well and it means so much that you would be here and bring Topaz to share his love for our son and our family. And how can I ever thank you for what you have done with Sharif, the time he spent with you yesterday has helped tremendously with him dealing with this, I don't know how I could ever repay you," and she began to weep, Mr. Rudolphson nodded in agreement as he comforted his wife. My mom said, "There is no need for that, we are in this together, I couldn't have dreamt up a better family to befriend our child, he loves you guys and so do we and there is nothing that we won't do to help you through this, you are good, strong parents and you have been amazing through this trial, God sees and he knows his people and he always aligns us with each other." Mrs. Rudolphson grabbed Mama J in an embrace and said, "Bless you, Topaz said you always know what needs to be heard."

I was just standing there and I could feel my knees becoming a little wobbly, it was all becoming a bit too real at this point. Mr. Rudolphson said, "Come on over here son and gimme some love, how are you feeling?" He pulled me over and embraced me, I was shaking like a leaf as I said, "I'm okay." I then went over to Sharif and said, "Wassup," he just looked up at me and said, "I can't do it LT, I can't go in there and see him laying in that box." Tears welled up in his eyes as he grabbed a hold of both my hands and said, "This is terrible, it's terrible, I'm upsetting my parents because I can't get it together, what kinda man is that." I said, "Rif, that's nonsense. Your parents aren't upset, they understand these things, they would never get upset with you about anything like this. And as far as being a man, I have no questions about your manhood and you shouldn't either." He looked up and gave a slight devilish grin. I said, "Now, I got your back and I'm standing here, do you want to try going in here with me or do you want to sit here and I'll be right back." He said, "I'ma man up and go with you, I can't let you go by yourself." He stood up and grabbed me by the hand, he turned toward our parents and he said, "Mr. Jesper, we got each other's back and we goin' in here a see my Baby Bro. Dad it's time for me to man up, my bro is waitin' to see me." Tears ran down Mr. Rudolphson's face as Sharif leaned over and kissed his mom on the cheek. He then said, "Mrs. Jesper don't worry, I got him." He then kissed Mama J on the cheek, Papa J's eyes welled up as he put his fist up and said, "Very good young man, very good." Papa J then embraced Mama J. Both sets of parents watched intensely as we entered the room hand in hand slowly and approached the coffin where Tylique's body laid

looking as much like an angel as I have ever seen.

You hear people say it but he literally looked like he

was in a peaceful sleep. I could feel Sharif's grip

tightening, as he wept, he said, "I couldn't save him

LT, I couldn't." I had tears but strangely enough I

was standing strong on my two feet for a change, it

was as though the grief wasn't enough to take me and

Sharif down together, but one on one was a different

ball game all together, and everyday I was dealing

with the situation a little better. After about

twenty minutes of standing there Sharif shook my arm

and said, "Alright, I'm good we can go." He looked

over and said, "I love you Bro. I'm sorry but I'm

gonna do right by him, I promise." I looked at

Sharif, he cracked a half of a grin and he led me away

from the coffin. As we approached the doorway our

parents had moved off to the side of entrance, as soon

as we emerged from the room the first face I saw was

Whalid. He just stared with an empty look as if he

didn't know what to say, as I got closer I focused in

and seen Christine and Jeremi, I was not amused.

Whalid came up and introduced himself, Christine and

Jeremi to Sharif and told him he was sorry about his
lost.  He then said, "Can I borrow my brother from you
for a few moments?"  Sharif said, "Absolutely, but
don't be long, I want to introduce you to some of my
cousins that are here from other places."  Whalid
said, "I won't keep him long playa, I will make it
quick."  I interrupted, "We'll make it quicker than
that, I can talk to Whalid anytime, Rif take me where
you were, now."  Whalid's eyebrows raised up so high
on his forehead I thought they were going to touch his
hairline.  Christine looked puzzled, Jeremi had his
normal simple smug look that he has perfected and
Sharif looked a little thrown off by how I shut Whalid
down but he listened and said, "I'm sorry man, we
won't be long."  I followed Sharif's lead and went on
to meet a few of his family members, each one was
pretty nice and welcoming and seemed to already know
of my existence, it was a little awkward, but not in a
creepy way.  I could see Whalid and Jeremi's eyes
following us throughout the room, I knew Whalid was
becoming more and more irritated by the moment, but I
didn't care, I couldn't imagine that there was

anything that he had to say that I would be interested in.

As the viewing winded down and the people began to slowly leave I told Sharif, "I better grab my parents up, you know it's past their bedtime and I didn't drive my car." He said, "If you're not ready to go you don't have to Boo, I will take you home later, I'd rather have you with me right now." I leaned my head slightly to the right and said, "Boo, seriously Rif." He said, "Don't do that, go on over and let your peeps know that I'm gonna drop you off a bit later." I didn't even argue, I just went over and explained to Mama and Papa J that I would be along later. Of course Mama J responded, "Okay Baby, don't be too late, running around with Mr. Sharif, he needs to get some rest too before the funeral tomorrow." I said, "Yes ma'am." I walked with them to the car and seen them off. On my way back to the funeral to meet back up with Sharif I ran into Whalid and Jeremi while they were going to Whalid's truck. Whalid immediately started in on me, "Oh so you just didn't find time to talk to me at all, is that what went on here Eugene. Or is Eugene not around anymore, cause it seems that ever since your name changed, I don't know you no more."  I said, "Don't start with me Whalid, I have nothing to say to you, you don't know how to talk to people and I will not waste my time arguing with you, it's not worth it."  He became very tense and said, "Bitch you didn't even let me say anything, you don't know what I was gonna say.  I was trying to console you, but you think you are the shit all of a sudden. How are you the shit sitting around with the family of a nigga that didn't give a fuck about you?"  I felt myself becoming very upset, as I responded, "You don't know what the fuck you're talking about; you know nothing about what Ty and I shared, you disrespectful jerk.  Where's your girlfriend at, you should occupy your time with her and your intentions for her." Jeremi chimed in, "If he cared so much about you how did we both have him, you are so fuckin' dumb."  I spun around and said, "Cum swallowing bitch, do you want me to pop you in your pie hole again?"  He responded, "Oh Bitch, don't get it fucked up, it won't go the same way as last time, and I owe you anyway, so don't get it fucked up."  I stood firm and said, "You heard what I said, you can dish out all the threats you want, but if you keep talking to me - I promise you - they will be needing to do a double ceremony tomorrow, so keep talking at your own risk." Jeremi went to say something else as Whalid interrupted him and said, "Shut the fuck up J, I told you don't start that shit; you're never gonna put your hands on him and I told you that, so just shut the fuck up! T you just need to stop with the shady bullshit; when I'm talking to you - you will listen, the same way that Christine does; you asked me where she was; she went to get the car for us like I told her to. She's obedient, just like you will be, do you understand?" He stood and looked at me like he was seriously waiting on an answer. After a moment I said, "What you need to understand is that, I have nothing to say to either one of you, and all that trying to control me - Please! You can kiss my ass and bark at the hole!" With that I walked away and left the two of them standing there, a few steps away I could see Sharif awaiting my return. As I approached him he said, "Alright, is everything okay with moms and pops? I said, "Yes, they are cool, they said for us not to stay out too long." He said, "No problem." A few seconds later a car came screeching up in front of the funeral home and out jumps Nati with her and Ty's daughter. She ran up to Sharif and said, "Am I too late." Sharif shrugged his shoulders and said, "I'm not sure." She stormed through the doors and into the funeral home, I looked at Rif and said, "Is she always this ridiculous?" He shook his head yes and we both just chuckled. A short time later Mr. Rudolphson came escorting Nati out of the building, she was becoming a little loud, "How can they say that they aren't going to reopen the coffin for me and my daughter, that's bullshit and you know it!" He replied, "Nati, I have told you time after time, I am not the one for all that smart talking and yelling, I don't like it, and it's disrespectful. And this is not the time for all that." She stopped on the steps, stared at me and said, "Well being as though we are saying what's not needed; why is he here?" Sharif chimed in, "He has just as much right to be here as you do!" She yelled, "Sharif, shut up, you don't know nothin' you are always tryin' to add your bullshit and nobody gives a shit." Sharif's eyes got extremely big and his eyebrows raised up really high as he said, "Nati you smut, I will choke you out!  If you say one more thing smart to any member of this family I swear on my brother, I'ma take you out!"  She just stood there for a moment looking very combative, she then responded, "I don't know why I ever involved myself with this weird ass family; y'all are literally sitting around acting like this faggot is a part of your family and like he has some right to be involved, it's not right and y'all are fuckin' confused."  Then in a very stern voice Mrs. Rudolphson emerged from the front door of the funeral home and said, "Nobody is confused here but you Nati.  You aggravated my son while he was alive with your ranting and raving and acting foolish. You and him were finished a long time ago; there is no need for an opinion from you on who he dealt with after your time was up.  And no one cares what your take is on our family.  There's one thing that you need to know about our family that is an absolute fact – you are not a part of the family unit and your daughter always will be no matter what you do or say, so be respectful and leave now before I have to come out of my comfort zone and unleash things unto you that I have been longing to give you since I met you."

Nati didn't say another word, she went back and got into the car that she came in and they drove away.

I said, "I'm so sorry, I didn't' mean to be trouble or the subject of any drama." Mrs. Rudolphson said, "Nonsense, that girl is a problem and has always been; I never approved of her, she's messy. Topaz you have just as much right to be here as anyone else that loved Tylique and you are a part of our family, period." She looked over at Mr. Rudolphson and said, "I'm tired, and I'm ready to go home." He grabbed her hand and led her away the building and toward their parked car, she turned and said, "Be careful and I will see you guys in the morning." I gave a confident wave as the Rudolphsons entered their car.

Sharif said, "Are you hungry, I can take you to get something to eat." I said, "I am actually, can we get pizza?" He smiled and said, "You can have whatever you want LT. And don't let that bitch Nati bother you, if she steps out of line, cuss that hoe out." I replied as I got into Sharif's black 2004 Cadillac Eldorado, "I'm not worried about her, as long as she doesn't touch me, we are good, she can say whatever she wants." He responded, "Well, if you're alright with it I will try to be, but I'm not promising anything." He then pulled out his cell phone and called the pizza shop and ordered our food for pick up, I laughed and said, "You knew the number by heart, do you come here much?" He laughed and said, "Ty always said you were a smart ass."

Once we got to the restaurant I didn't get out of the car, I felt a little uneasy about being out with just he and I, so I let Sharif go in and pick up the food, I was just about exhausted anyway. Sharif is really well known in the community and well respected, there was no need for me to feel uneasy being with him. The seats in Sharif's car were already in a leaning position and they were the softest leather that you have ever felt. Also the windows were tinted to perfection and before I knew it I had drifted off to sleep. As I lay there I was feeling a little heated all of a sudden as I opened my eyes I was caught off guard by Sharif's hand rubbing my inner thigh, I grabbed his hand and said, "What are we doing Rif?" He replied, "Rubbing on a sexy specimen and getting' horny as fuck, what about you, whatchu doin' LT?" I grabbed his hand and replied, "I'm getting confused here. This is not supposed to be happening, did you forget our agreement?" He sat back in his seat and said, "I thought about that arrangement, and I want to show you what I think now about that. Lean over here please…" against my better judgment I did it and all I felt in the next moment was his tongue infiltrating my mouth like a fortress that he planned on conquering. I was a little shocked at how comfortable he seemed to be with the flow of feelings involving me. It was like there was no confusion involved with his choice of sexuality, but I knew that couldn't possibly be so; not this soon. I truly believe this is a case of being hot and horny and not built on much more than that, I couldn't let myself fall into this trap, but I definitely did not want to hurt Rif's feelings. I was definitely regretting the earlier events of the day at this point. I tried to pull away from him but it wasn't working, I don't know if it was his grip on me or the fact that my body was as entrenched in lust as his was. I know what I need to do but like clockwork I can feel myself falling into this forbidden zone yet again. Finally the kiss broke and I said, "What the hell Rif, this is a mess," he interrupted me, "Why, why is it a mess.  It feels right to me."  I said, "How do you know it is right, how do I know you are not just horny, and trying to get off and using me as a vehicle by which to get your stuff off."  His eyebrow raised up as if he was becoming impatient with the whole situation, as he answered, "You don't know, but you are gonna have to trust me LT!  Are you telling me that you can't trust me, all of a sudden I'm not worth trusting, are you serious right now."  I could see the hurt forming in his eyes.  I grabbed his hands and said, "Okay Sharif, I'm not trying to be hurtful, but I'm afraid things won't work and I don't want to lose your friendship, because if it doesn't work out, what are the chances that we will remain close?"  He said, "I'm making a choice here for my life all about you, how can you just leave me hangin', what kinda' shit is that?"  I said, "Boy, I'm not leaving you hanging, I just don't want to be hurt and left alone when this is all over with, I don't think I could stand it, especially when my first decision was not to indulge."  He yelled, "But you did didn't you, you did indulge.  I wasn't fuckin' myself early this morning, or was that not you that was laying underneath me!" I said, "Don't yell at me Rif, I'm not trying to…" he cut me off, "You're not tryin' to what; to fuck wit' me! Was the dick bad for you or something, is there something that you're not telling me?" I said, "No, that's not it, but speaking of that, you said that's the first time you've had an experience – you didn't even give yourself a chance to process it, are you sure that this is even for you." He replied, "Stop saying that, I did process it, and yes you are for me." I said, "Okay but what about that apparent attraction that you have for females, what are you gonna do about that, because I don't share." A smile appeared on his face as he replied, "And neither do I. So I guess we are finally gettin' on the same page – now can I have a kiss and can we go eat pizza before the shit needs micro-waved?"

We went over his house, his parents had already gone to bed and all of the house guests that were staying at their house had pretty much made their way to bed as well. We were very quiet as we made our way to Sharif's room, we were just getting seated when there was a slight tap on the door. Sharif went and

answered it, it was his cousin Tony, I was introduced
to earlier this evening at the viewing; he had flown
in from Florida for the funeral with his mom and
little sister. Tony was an extremely attractive
eighteen year old with an adorable southern draw when
he spoke. I noticed that he looked very nice in his
shirt and slacks earlier, but now that he was standing
in the doorway with a tank top and shorts on I could
see that he had a body that would not quit. He was
caramel colored, about six foot tall and deep brown
eyes; his face was perfectly framed with the sexiest
little goatee, he was very pleasant to the eye. He
asked Sharif could he come in and chill for awhile,
since everyone else was going to sleep. Sharif asked,
"Hey LT, do you mind if Tony chills with us." I said,
"Absolutely not, come on Tony we got pizza, have
some." He said, "I don't mind if I do, Lil dude. I
usually don't eat this kinda junk food, but hell, why
not." Sharif chimed in, "Yeah, he's a gym rat, how
many days a week are you in the gym now cuz?" He
answered proudly, "Everyday when I can, but at least
five. You know I gotta keep my shit tight for the
honeys." He and Sharif chuckled and we all continued

enjoying the pizza, we were enjoying each others company when Tony got his nerve up and said, "So lil dude, can I ask you a question?" I said, "Sure." He continued, "So you're gay is that correct?" I said, "Yes, that's correct." He had a strange kind of a look on his face, very inquisitive. I said, "Why do you ask that Tony?" he replied, "Oh, I could just tell, when I met you earlier, and even before Rif introduced us, I could tell you were a little light in the loafers." Sharif jumped in abruptly, "Yo cuzzo, don't say no ole disrespectful shit to Topaz, we don't play that." He quickly replied, "No, no I wasn't tryna' be smart, I'm sorry if you took it that way. It's just that I ain't never been around a gay dude, but you seem mad cool. Only thing is you kinda' act like a girl, and it is trippin' me out, cause it's not like some of them dudes I see back at home. They are all loud and some of them wear girl's clothes all the time - I don't understand." I replied, "That's a very complicated part of the gay life Tony, everyone doesn't do those things, the homosexual community is filled with a lot of interesting folks who express their individuality in a ton of ways." Sharif just

sat back and listened as the conversation continued, I
was pretty unbothered by his interrogation, I found it
a bit funny actually, he was truly a bit clueless on
the subject, I thought he must be living in a bubble
down in Florida.  The more questions I answered the
more personal they became, eventually he reached the
topic of sex, and he took a deep breath and blurted
out, "So dig this, one of my boys admitted to me that
he let this cat give him some dome, I don't know why
he did it?"  Sharif interrupted, "Because it wasn't
none of your business, that's why you didn't
understand."  Tony said, "Shut up Rif, I'm serious.
Lil dude, why do you think that dudes let y'all suck
them off and shit?"  I leaned my head slightly to the
right and said, "Well first off, what makes you think
that I would be able to answer that, have you've
pegged me as a dick-sucker?  Wouldn't that be more of
a question for your poor friend that you felt was
being taken advantage of.  Because that is how you
feel, if I'm hearing you right – you feel like your
friend was taken advantage of by the gay guy that gave
him head, or did I hear you wrong?"  A blank look took
over Tony's handsome face for a second and then he

replied, "Well kind of." I sat straight up on the edge of Sharif's bed and said, "Explain yourself, explain how do you feel that your friend was a victim, what did your friend lose in that situation?" Sharif said, "Yeah, I'm listening to you cuzzo, but you ain't makin' no sense. It sounds like your road-dog likes to get his dick sucked and he didn't care who sucked it as long as he got his nut. And then he was cool with it because he felt comfortable enough to share it with you." Tony was quiet for a moment, I could imagine that he was probably a little embarrassed at this point. The conversation had taken a shift, where it started kind of cool and the nature was one of trying to gain understanding on the subject, it had now started to feel like a slight attack and I was assured of that when Tony said, "So tell me Lil dude; you were involved with my cousin Ty right?" I said, "Absolutely." He said, "So did you use to suck his dick?" Sharif jumped in and said, "Yo dog, not cool!" I said, "No, it's okay Sharif; let me explain something to you about me and your cousin. There was nothing casual about the relationship between me and Ty, we were a couple, he loved me and I loved him. So to answer your question, did I use to suck his dick; I did whatever he required to keep him sexually satisfied." A look of shock was evident on Tony's face, he then said, "Okay, so you like suckin' niggas dicks though!" I replied, "That's not what I said, I have never had a casual sex act in my life, I have only ever had sex with someone that I cared about who in return cared about me too. I hope that kind of sheds some light on who I am for you, though I get the feeling that it won't." He said, "Why you say that, man." I said, "Because I've been speaking with you, but you haven't been listening, you've been more or less firing insults at me, on the sly." He apologized and swore that he didn't mean it that way, but I wasn't buying the apology. I kept a cool head with it because I could see Sharif's attitude stirring. I was really in no mood for an altercation of any kind, I just wanted this conversation to end. Shortly after that conversation fizzled out Tony said he was tired and he went to bed. I sat there for a little longer talking with Sharif before he decided to drive me home.

On the way to my house he said, " I don't know what got into Tony, he was trippin' and it really sounded like he had something that he was trying to hide. That was so crazy, I don't even know what he was getting at, that was just dumb." I said, "I don't either but I know an attack when I see one. And he got very close to making me lose my cool." I laid back in my seat and relaxed as Sharif drove, he looked over and said, "Damn, are you comfortable." I laughed and said, "Like you wouldn't believe. It seems like everytime I sit here I wanna go to sleep." He said, "Cause you know I got you." I said, "Oh, is that what that is! You are so cocky sometimes, it's funny but it kinda works for you." He said, "I don't think I'm cocky, I just know how to get what I want, so, do I have you at this point or what?" I looked over and said, "Sharif, at this point are you taking no for an answer?" He replied, "Not at all!" I said, "Well I'm all yours, please don't make me regret it. But let me say this, for some strange reason, I'm not worried, I definitely believe that you are going to do right by me. But I am not sure about our parents; I already know that Mama J is not going to approve, but she will

come around, I don't know what my dad is gonna say.
And I am terrified of what your parents are going to
think of me." He said, "Don't worry about none of
that Luv; it doesn't matter what anyone thinks but us,
period." I replied, "But come on Rif, it does leave
me looking a little slutty. Dating the brother of
your lover who has passed away and literally no time
has gone by. And in addition, the brother was
straight as an arrow; oh yeah, sounds like the work of
a slut to me." He interrupted me, "But that is not
how it all went down!" I replied, "I know Rif, but to
the naked eye, that is how it looks. But for you, I
will endure, I think we are getting ready to travel
some rough road Mr. Rudolphson." He said, "Don't
worry, we will be fine, I promise!"

We pulled up to the front of my house and Sharif
parked the car and turned off the ignition, he turned
his head to me and said, "What I need you to do is
concentrate on being happy. Can you do that LT?" I
said, "I can, I'm not going to worry anymore, I'm
gonna just roll with you and trust you." He smiled
and replied, "That's all I ask. Because once your
happy then you will definitely keep me happy." He

took my hand and said, "So is there a chance that I can sleep with you tonight? I really would like to have you close to me right through here." I replied, "I'm sorry but I'm not in a sexing kind of mood tonight Rif." He said, "I guess that's a good thing because neither am I, I didn't ask you for fuck time, I asked you to slumber with me, there's a difference. So Topaz J can I get a lil' comfort from my shawty tonight or what?" I smiled and responded, "Absolutely Papi." As we exited the car and started toward the house I thought about how interesting of a person that Sharif Rudolphson is; he has such a hard edge to him, but then when you really get to know him you realize that he is big cream puff. He is very passionate about the people and the things that he cares about. It made me smile to know that I was one of those things. In the far corner of my mind is the reality of the situation; in my heart of hearts I know that this isn't going to work out, but my I still have that little dysfunction that shows up and makes me weak to a love interest; one day I will have to talk to Mama J about that, but not today.

We went right into the house and proceeded downstairs to the gameroom, I turned on the television and told Sharif to have a seat and chill while I get everything that we needed to be comfortable. He took a seat on the couch and off I went to fetch a few pillows and blankets for us. While I was upstairs on the second floor I took a shower and put on a pair of pajamas, I also grabbed a pair of pajama bottoms for Sharif out of Whalid's old room. On my way back down the hallway I could hear the signal for a text message going off on my cell phone, I grabbed my phone off of my bed and started back down the stairs to the gameroom. I looked at my phone and there were several messages from Jay-Jay and a couple from Whalid, I immediately checked out Jay-Jay's messages, he was trying to see how I felt and also the information about the funeral time. I responded back to him with a text of the information and also informed him that I would talk to him soon. Whalid's text I simply didn't read at that time, I reached the gameroom to find a very cute and very sleep Sharif laying on the couch. I layed a blanket over him, I didn't want to disturb him, he was so peaceful, it just wouldn't have been right.   I spread a comforter on the floor for myself and laid down, I decided to watch a little television until I fall off to sleep, as I laid there I was curious as to what Whalid had to say in his texts.   I opened my phone to find four messages of him ranting and raving; his normal.   He went on and on about how he didn't appreciate me ignoring him or the way I spoke to him and Jeremi.   The last message said, 'You act like you don't want me, if that is true, let me know so I can put Jeremi in your place.   It's up to you!'   In light of that foolish comment, I turned off the television and my phone and went to sleep.   I felt Sharif join me on the comforter around 4am, he was trying to wake me up and that was evident, his whole body was a little damp.   He had taken a shower and didn't thoroughly dry off, the funny part is, I heard him when he went into the bathroom and cut the shower on.   He pulled up close to me and whispered in my ear, "LT are you sleep?"   I said, "Yup."   He responded, "Alright, but I need you woke for this."   I said, "For what."   In a matter of seconds I was stripped naked and placed into some form of a Karma Sutra pose.   I laughed to myself because I knew that I was this flexible but had no idea how in the hell Rif got that flexible or knew about any of this exotic sexing. But rest assure, I was going to ask questions but right now I was going to give in to the tingling that was running throughout my body as Sharif worked in a steady motion. He was doing a good job of being quiet and just grunting and groaning, me on the other hand, it took everything I had to keep from yelling out in ecstasy.

As the episode rolled to a close, I was completely worn out, my legs were rubbery, my breathing was a bit heavy and I was concentrating really hard not to let Sharif see the state that he had left me in. He said, "Come on Luv, lay next to me, I'm fucked up right now, I'm tired as hell, you alright?" I said, "I'm fine Papi…" he interrupted, "You better stop that shit, when you call me Papi, it turns me on; I don't know why. When I was waiting for you to come back down to the gameroom I was trying to figure out why I was on brick, it happened as soon as you called me Papi in the car. So watch yourself with that." I said, "Wow, I will be sure to stay mindful of that Papi." He laughed and pulled me in to him, planted a seriously deep kiss on me and round two was in progress.

By 7:30am Sharif and I said our I love yous and see ya laters and he was headed home. I was wondering why my parents weren't up and stirring around, when I got to the second floor it was totally quiet. Then just as I went to turn into my room I heard something that stopped me in my tracks, it was coming from my parents room, I proceeded down the hallway and before I got all the way to their bedroom door I was immediately transformed into an immature 12 year old. I was disgusted and taken off guard, the bed was squeaking and the moans and groans were escaping the room. I did what any 12 year old would do, I said, "Ew," under my breath and quickly tip-toed back to my room and acted like it didn't happen. I guess it's true, no child wants to know that their parents still have sex. It's kind of funny when you think about it, my reaction was as though I was so innocent and untouched, when meanwhile I was probably doing worse just two floors below not long ago, that really took nerve on my part, I had to laugh at myself.

By 9:45am our house was in full swing we had all showered, eaten breakfast and were dressed in our clothes for the funeral. Papa J was sitting in his chair in the livingroom speaking about us leaving at 10 a.m. since the church was not that far away from our house, when the phone rang. Mama J answered the phone, after a few seconds she was smiling and I could tell right away from her responses that it was Mrs. Rudolphson on the other end of the line. Mama J said, "Okay Hun, we'll see you shortly, and thanks again." She hung up and said, "Topaz that was Mrs. Rudolphson; they are about 5 minutes away and they would like for you to ride in the limo with the family. They will be here to get you shortly. That is so nice of them, the way they include you into their family and they are so genuine, it makes me love them even more; they are a beautiful couple." Papa J nodded in agreement.

I went out to the hallway and took a final look in the mirror at my custom made black suit accompanied with a black on black printed silk shirt and tie; I was definitely looking my best. Within moments I could see the black limousine pulling up outside, I told my parents that the Rudolphsons were here and I would see them at the church; I then proceeded out of the door and down the walkway to the beautiful black stretch limousine. As I approached, the door was opened by the driver, who was ever so polite and asked me, "How are you this morning son?" I replied, "I am very good, thanks!" As soon as I looked forward the first face I saw was Sharif, he cracked a bit of a smile, but I could see all of the tension in his face. Next I seen Mr. and Mrs. Rudolphson, they were smiling and welcoming me into their presence, while Sharif was reaching for my hand to lead me to have a seat next to him. As I sat I said, "Good morning everyone, thank you for having me in your company, I can't voice how appreciative I am right now, thank you." Mrs. Rudolphson smiled and then introduced me to both, her parents and Mr. Rudolphson's parents, and strangely enough they all knew who I was. As we were riding to the church Mrs. Rudolphson said, "Topaz, I would love it if you would sing something this morning, we didn't add it to the program because originally I thought it may be too much on you, but seeing how you are handling everything, I would love to hear your voice this morning; only if you feel up to it." I said, "If that's what you would like me to do, I will do it, I'm more than happy to sing." Mr. Rudolphson's mom said, "My daughter-in-law said you have the voice of an angel." I didn't know how to respond, I just smiled, as Sharif said jokingly, "He's aight!" I hit his leg and said, "Don't start." He laughed and said, "Just jokes, just jokes." I rolled my eyes and laughed, as did everyone else in the limo. It wasn't a very long ride, we reached the church pretty quickly and the limo pulled up in front of the church, the driver got out and came around to open the door for us to exit the vehicle. As I got out I was amazed; I had never seen anything like this scene, there were tons of people and media outside the church, there were camereas flashing like crazy and video being shot by all the major networks from our area and even the Jackson College area. I'm more than sure that had to do with the nature of Tylique's death. It was violent and senseless, and he was not a part of the actual altercation that erupted into this tragedy. Ty was at Jackson College on an athletic scholarship, he had a very positive future - unfortunately, he never even got to attend one class, and it was no fault of his own. When you think about it, it really was a sad state of affairs.

As we walked into the church and took in the sea of familiar faces that filled the pews, all sorts of emotions were taking place. Both sets of grandparents and Mr. and Mrs. Rudolphson led the way, Sharif and I were walking side by side directly behind them and behind us was a slew of cousins, uncles and aunts. We proceeded down front and filled the front pews. It was really too real sitting there in front of the ivory and gold casket and knowing that the love of my life was actually laying in there. Once everyone was seated and calm the lid of the coffin was lifted and there was my angel lying still like in a bad dream that I could awake from. I took a few deep breaths and just held onto Sharif's hand, which was now cold, clammy and shaking. I looked him in his eyes and said, "Are you with me, are you alright." He nodded yes. The service began, and there were so many people that poured out messages of peace and love to the family. Jackson College's full Board of directors were present and they all came to the front as the school's President spoke. He expressed his deepest sympathy for the family and their loss, his speech was very heart felt. The church was very quiet as the speakers came and went you could hear a little sniffling, but it was otherwise quiet. There was a member of the congregation reading off sympathy cards that had been mailed directly to the church, I was listening but totally preoccupied with the amount of flowers that were sent, it was like something from a movie, I don't think I've ever seen that many flowers on the inside of a building. There were such nice things being said about Tylique, he was truly a well-liked person who was taken away too soon. As I continued zoning out and scanning the crowd, I could feel Sharif squeezing my hand, his hand was so cold and clammy – he really wasn't taking this so well. I leaned over and whispered in his ear, "Don't worry Baby, it will all be over soon." He just looked at me and his eyes were a bit empty, I said, "How 'bout when I go up to sing you come and stand with me and help me out, I'm really nervous." I was a little nervous but I figured, if he is focused on taking care of me it will take the strain off of him temporarily. He cracked a weak smile and whispered, "I gotchu Luv, don't worry, you're goin' tear it up, Ty will be able to hear you from heaven." That put a smile on my face and the nervousness actually went away.

Next up to the podium was Mrs. Rudolphson; her husband escorted her from her seat. She was wearing a beautiful white suit heavily adorned with lace, rhinestones and bugle beads on the lapel. The skirt framed her legs as if it was made right onto her body; she accompanied her suit with a 4 inch white peep-toed heel. Mr. Rudolphson was matched to perfection in a white double-breast suit with a perfect "Wise Guys" fit; it laid flawlessly on his well built frame. The pair of them were absolutely stunning. As she took her place in the pulpit behind the podium the church went into dead silence. She began to speak with her voice crackling from the tears she was holding back, "I don't have the words to say as to how I feel about the fact that each and every person here took time out to come and celebrate my baby. The outpouring of love from our community and Jackson College is something I've only heard about, I've never witnessed it, but on today I can say there were other people who loved my son. And that's a good feeling, especially after the way he was taken from us.  We, his parents, we dressed in white today instead of black.  I don't want to be in mourning, I've done that all week – all week, do you hear me!  Praise God, I've mourned his passing and I'm tired, Lord, I'm so tired, I can't cry anymore.  I don't have a reason, because I know that my baby is resting with the Lord!"  She stepped back and began to shout out to the Lord in praise, simultaneously praise shouting started to fill the sanctuary.  Sharif had completely broken down at this point and had his head in my lap sobbing.  Within roughly ten minutes order had been regained and Mrs. Rudolphson continued, "There is a family here today that are recent friends of ours.  Can Mr. and Mrs. Jesper please stand up so all of my family and friends can see you.  This man and woman of God have been an absolute blessing to us in our time of grief.  They have been a beacon of light in this dark – dark time of life.  They are a couple that jumped in and sat in the parent roles until our parents arrived, you see –  I'm a grown woman, but when I got the news that my child's life had been extinguished, all I wanted was my Mama!!!!!  And in an instant The Lord sent me The Jespers.  And they allowed us to lean on them until and after my Mama got to town, y'all don't hear me!!!!! I said, this man and woman who are the parents of one of my child's friends, they didn't really know us on a deep scale of friendship, we were merely joined by the love shared between our children. This God sent couple opened their arms with no hesitation and said, 'Come to me, Lean on me, Cry on my shoulder, What is it that you need, What can I do to ease the pain?' Y'all don't understand what I'm telling you! I was wallowing in my grief to the point that I have another child that I couldn't help him through his grief - My baby was lost and I couldn't reach him, OH GOD, I couldn't get hold of my child and fix what was troubling him, My Lord. The Jespers reached down and grabbed Sharif and pulled him up from his despair. They have been a set of angels to us and we are forever grateful. After this Going Home Ceremony ends we will be going over to the Phillyankos Hall for fellowship and a fully catered meal, everyone here is welcome. This was also handled solely by the Jespers and they insisted that they take care of it, the preparation and financial burden, they said they wanted to do it in honor of our son and to take the burden away from our family of having to prepare a meal on this day. So I say to you Mr. and Mrs. Jesper - We love you, We appreciate you and we couldn't have made it through this without all of your love and compassion, God Bless You!" She blew a kiss at my parents, and I swear there wasn't a dry eye in the place, it was really a heart wrenching moment, I was trying really hard not to get started with the crying but it was just about impossible. I lifted Sharif's head from my lap and said, "It's cool Rif, it's cool, you're doing fine, okay." He responded with a head nod. I put my attention on my parents and my Uncle Joe, Jay-Jay and his boyfriend Quan were sitting right next to them in the pew on their left and on the right side of them was Whalid, Christine and Jeremi. Whalid had a few tears welled up in his eyes along with a small look of confusion; while Jeremi had a dead lock stare and look of contempt on his face, I refused to even give into the thought of those two on this day. I looked back to the pulpit as Mrs. Rudolphson continued, "And speaking of love, the next person that you all are going to hear from is a person who, without a doubt, absolutely loved and shared a special bond with my baby. He has become a member of our family, we are just crazy about him, he is the youngest son of the Jespers, his name is Topaz and I thank God that he sent him to us. When I was at one of my lowest points, my Topaz; I hope you don't mind us borrowing him from time to time Mrs. Jesper." She took a moment to chuckle and she and Mama J exchanged smiles; she continued, "I was really losing it a bit and this child shared with me a talent that I had no idea was laid on him so heavily, Ty would talk about Short Stuff, as he would call him, singing. But my God, the soothing sound of comfort that came out of his mouth turned the whole thing around. I felt like arms had wrapped me in the bosom of the Divine One, it was undeniable. The anointing that lies within you my sweetheart is undeniable. I want you to come up here and share that anointing this morning if you would, I know I can use it."

I stood up and at the same time Sharif stood in unison like two perfect black dominoes, as we made our way to the pulpit I started to notice a lot of people that I had no idea were there, I could feel the tears building up in my eyes. Amongst the crowd was my friends from school, Akai, Rebecca, Michelle and Nichelle - it meant so much that they actually came, our friendship is very new, I was beside myself with the fact that they drove 2 hours to get here, that gives them a huge boost with me in the credibility department. Also I could see Nati, Angie, TriAnn and a guy who wasn't really familiar to me, I figured it must be her fiancé, Sam. When our eyes locked she shot me a swift dirty look and rolled her eyes up into her head. For the first time, it actually didn't bother me, I expected such from my sister, I doubt that she'll ever change. I turned my attention to Mr. and Mrs. Rudolphson, they were completely in anticipation of the two of us reaching the podium, they both had smiles on the faces. When we reached them like clockwork I embraced Mrs. Rudolphson and Sharif embraced his dad, he then stood on my right side as I approached the microphone. I cleared my throat and I began, "I know we've heard a lot about Ty this morning, but I can tell you without a doubt, it is all true, he was just an awesome being. And that happens when you have awesome parents, from the first day that I came in contact with the Rudolphson Family I have been comfortable, loved and treated like one of their own, you don't find that everywhere. Trust me, I know of what I speak. When Mrs. Rudolphson asked me to sing she didn't say what she wanted me to do," I turned to her and then I continued, "She told me to do whatever God laid on my heart and it would be perfect. Well from that time 'til now all I have been thinking about is how lucky I was to have the time with Tylique that God allotted me. How merciful was that to give me a friend, a true friend who cared about me the way that I cared about him. God's grace never disappoints, not ever…" I started to choke up. Mr. Rudolphson stepped up and grabbed my shoulders and said, "You can do it son, it's okay." I said, "I'm sorry everyone, but it hurts, I know he is with the Lord, but the absence hurts, it's selfish of me, but I miss my friend. But I thank you God for the little time, I thank you!" Sharif grabbed my hand and I focused on my mom, she gave me a head nod and I began to sing slowly…

Great is your mercies towards me…

Your love a kindness towards me…

Your tender mercies, I see…

Day after day.

Forever faithful towards me…

You're always providing for me…

Great is your mercies I see…

Great is your great.

I started back into the verse and the church's choir and musicians joined in. At that point I got very comfortable and allowed my feelings to overflow into the song. By the time I reached the last verse of the song the church was in an uproar, people were shouting and singing along and praising God freely. The rush of emotions overtook me and I dropped my head and stop singing as the tears flowed freely from my eyes. I lifted my free hand to cue the musicians to take the volume of their playing down low and the choir to sing softly, Sharif continued to hold onto my right hand tightly, he just sobbed as I sang the last verse with all the feeling that was pinned up in my tiny body…

Great is your mercies towards me…

Your love a kindness towards me…

Your tender mercies, I see…

Day after day.

Forever faithful towards me…

You're always providing for me…

Great is your mercies I see…

Great is your great.

Sharif grabbed me in an embrace as I finished singing, I noticed Mr. Rudolphson helping Mrs. Rudolphson to her feet.  The four of us headed out of the pulpit as the musicians continued to play, the church was in a complete uproar, it took the pastor about fifteen minutes to regain control as the people praised loudly and freely.  I looked over and seen Mama J being comforted by Papa J and Whalid just staring at me.  Christine had tears in her eyes, while Jeremi sat looking confused about what had just gone on.  We took our seats as the choir continued chanting at a low roar, the pastor had taken his place back in the pulpit and he spoke, "This is a testiment to God's favor being placed in an unlikely place."  I immediately tuned in to what he was saying, as did Mama J, I could see it in her face.  He continued, "This young man is a carrying an anointing on him that seems to heavy to imagine, but when he opened his mouth the presence of God filled this place.

Hallelujah, you all felt it, you couldn't miss is, and

if you did, you need to throw yourself on the alter

and ask the Lord to reveal himself to you, because, HE

IS HERE!!!!!! Topaz, son come back up here if you

would, and help me give thanks to our Father." I

immediately rose to my feet and made my way back to

the pulpit, the pastor put his arm around my shoulder

and he said, "Follow me son and let's lead our people

into praise." He sang,

> The presence of the Lord is here.

> The presence of the Lord is here.

I chimed in,

> I feel it in the atmosphere.

The pastor sang,

Oh Jesus, I said, the presence of the Lord is here.

He continued singing the lead and I filled in

with ad libs and a soulful whaling that really got the

crowd going. As the song drew to a close, the pastor

looked at me and said, "Do you see that son, that is

the Lord's anointing, do you see how it filled this

place as soon as you begin to share your gift. It is

your duty to minister through song, your gift will

bring people to the Lord and give them a better life. All you have to do is keep sharing your gift, I promise you God is pleased with you son, he is pleased." Mama J was just holding her arms in the air and crying, everything that the pastor was saying were the same things that she has been saying to me all along about my voice.

The pastor completed the service and everyone headed out of the church to their vehicles to form a caravan to go to the grave site. As we exited the church I noticed the light dusting of a cool drizzle of rain. We got into the limo and everyone was a bit quiet, this part of the ceremony is one that I definitely wasn't looking forward to. To see them literally lower him into the ground, I shivered at the thought of it. Sharif was quiet but attentive to me as usual, I assured him I was okay. Mrs. Rudolphson sat quietly in her seat and as she and I made eye contact she nodded her head and said, "You did good Baby, real good, thank you." I just lowered my head. She said, "It's okay, Baby, I understand, I understand."

Before long we arrived at the grave site and began to get out of the limo. I noticed right away that the ground was a bit moist, which disgusted me, I definitely didn't want mud all over me, though this was truly not the time for me to pull out my diva card. Everyone gathered around the hole in the ground which was lined with what seemed to be red carpet, there were all types of contraptions that were in place to be able to lower the casket into the ground. As we stood waiting for the pastor to begin speaking, I noticed the aggravation in Nati's face as she tried whispering to TriAnn, "I can't stand these motherfuckers; they act just like me and my daughter don't matter and then act like this faggot is the shit." TriAnn said to her, "Nati, they did mention the baby in the eulogy. Now, that whole thing with Eugene's weird ass, that's just ridiculous." Sam cut their conversation short, he said, "C'mon y'all, not here, not now." I kept an eye contact with TriAnn so as to let her know that I knew what was being said, I was in no mood for her antics on this day.

The pastor finally took his spot and began speaking, everyone was really quiet other than a

little sniffling and crying. Once the reverand
finished his words they slowly began to lower the
coffin into the ground and like clockwork an outburst
ensued. "Oh God, No, No, No!!!!! Tylique!" We were
all in shock and just standing there stunned, this was
ridiculous, Nati had remained quiet through this whole
process and now all of a sudden she breaks out in this
fit of yelling and screaming. Somehow I knew it was
all a put on; she wanted her time to shine, it was so
desperate and so, so sad. She had handed her baby to
TriAnn before she started whooping and hollering. Sam
and TriAnn just watched her right along with the rest
of us, she was so loud, as she yelled, "He was mine,
he was the man of my dreams, he gave me a beautiful
child and now he's gone, he's gone!" She staggered
back and forth as the stunned onlookers hung on her
every word, as she continued, "He was my man, mines!"
As soon as she said that I am thinking to myself, 'Uh
oh, here we go!' She turned her attention right to
me, "You are nobody, and you weren't anybody to him,
you can tell people whatever you want. He was mine,
and he never stopped being mine. I couldn't keep him
away from you because you are nasty and freaky, you

bastard.  You had him confused, he wasn't your kind."

I looked at her and I refused to participate in this

dialogue, I just kept quiet and watched as she carried

on.  Sharif grabbed my hand and whispered in my ear,

"Hold on Luv, I…" I shook my head no, I didn't want to

be the center of this kind of attention, I didn't want

him arguing and fighting with her over me.  I figured

if I said nothing, the faster they could diffuse her

rant.  She went on, "Did you know that he never

stopped sleeping with me?  How bout that Eugene

Bailleau.  Yes that is the fag's real name, not Topaz

– it's Eugene!"  I immediately became infuriated, and

I was thinking to myself, 'It's a good thing she is on

the opposite side of that hole in the ground.'  She

continued on, "That's right he's not some great singer

and nice person, he is a filthy dick sucker and man

stealer, he tries to convince men that it's okay to

have gay sex with him, he's trifling!  Tylique told me

that he loved me and that he was done with that life,

we fucked all day long the day before he went away to

school and that nasty faggot must have been trying to

push up on him again when somebody killed him, you are

bad news you freak and you need to go away before

someone else gets hurt. Faggots are always bad luck, you Bitch!" She was making her way around to where I was, I had already told myself that if she gets to close, I'm going to have to apologize because I'm going to take her down. She was still yelling, "And what kind of family are you, cradling this queer, what's next you Sharif, you wanna put your dick in him next or are you already, you and Ty always wanted to do everything together. Did y'all fuck this faggot at the same time?" Sharif yelled back, "No, just you; you fuckin' smut!!!!!" You could feel a shift in the air as the rhythmic gasp of unbelief took place with his words. He continued, "Shut your mouth and shut it now before I…" she fired back, "Before you what motherfucker, what are you gonna do! You're sitting here holding the faggot's hand like now the Ty is dead the torch has been passed, so is he yours now, now you can have your turn with the homo." Sharif said, "He is family, and we care for him and that's what your problem is, nobody ever cared for you, you crazy whore." Her eyes grew so large and crazed as she screamed, "Was I a crazy whore when you fucked me the day after Tylique died, you couldn't wait to get this pussy without him being around, and for the record, his dick was always better." I couldn't believe what I was hearing, all sorts of emotions were spinning throughout my body, I had dropped Sharif's hand and hadn't even noticed that it was replaced with my Uncle Joe's, who was pulling me away from the two of them. Mr Rudolphson told Sharif to shut up, and he did so immediately. Mrs. Rudolphson was with the granparents who were trying to calm her down, she really wanted to get her hands on Nati, but they wouldn't let her loose. Nati continued ranting and raving, "Fuck all of you, and Sharif you know you are going to come and get at me, so shut the fuck up and stay away from the faggot before I have to fuck him up. I'm not sharing you with him too." Mr. Rudolphson turned toward Nati and yelled, "You shut your miserable fucking mouth, you two-bit family wrecking whore and get your sorry ass away from here and I mean now. Don't you dare disrespect my family in this way, we have let you carry on for the last time and I have had it!" Nati responded, "What's the problem, I'm trying to keep your other son on the straight and narrow; you should be thanking me." He yelled, "If you don't go ahead,

I'm gonna be choking you, now get going Nati, I'm serious, you've done enough damage here, go away, just go away." She said, "Fine, I will, I'm sick of this bullshit!" She proceeded to walk away from where we were standing and go back over to where TriAnn was standing with her baby and enjoying the drama, she had a wide grin on her face. Nati was moving swiftly around the grave and still beefing, "I'm tired of holding my tongue, this fucked up family is gonna know that I mean business, and that lil' fag too…" as she made her way over her high heeled shoe sank and slid in the moist grass and dirt causing her to lose her footing a bit. There were a few older women that were friends of the family that were standing nearby, they too felt as though Nati's behavior had been as ridiculous as could be and when she lost her footing they kind of chuckled. Well as she regained her step, she turned her wrath onto them, "What the fuck are you old bitches laughing at? You big fat, sloppy built bitches!" One of the women replied, "Little girl you were doing real well with the folks that you started this mess with, if you disrespect me again, God as my witness, I will make you swallow every tooth in your head. I have daughters your age and I don't play that mess!" The two other women standing next to her grabbed her and stopped her from getting to close to Nati. Nati said, "Oh please, let her go, do you feel froggish, then leap, cause I don't mind putting an old bitch on her back!" Things were really taking a turn for the worse; Nati continued her screaming and carrying on as the women worked on calming their friend down. One of the women turned and said, "Please Honey, this is not the time, nor the place for this, I beg you to just walk away and we will take her away, please Sister." Nati looked at her and said, "Don't you Honey/Sister me, with your ole convenient Christian bullshit. You old hoes kill me wit' that shit, now you're so holy, but are you that holy when you and that other Bitch are sucking each other's pussies! Y'all praising the Lord all day Sunday, and dyking all week long, Bitch everybody knows it." The woman turned her friend loose and said, "What did you say girl?" Nati continued, "Oh now you're dumb! Everybody knows about you fucking lesbians hiding behind those bibles; a bunch of old-ass dykes up in the church, no wonder y'all was so accepting of that faggot ass motherfucker, I hope y'all all catch AIDS and die, freak-ass motherfuckers." The woman lunged at Nati and grabbed her by the throat and the fight was on, it didn't last very long before the scuffle was broken up. Nati yelled, "Fuck this shit, I'ma see you Bitch," she made a swift turn around to walk away when she tripped on the red carpet outlining the grave and fell directly over into the hole on the side of the coffin. I couldn't believe that some folks actually broke out into laughter, it was a little funny but a bit scary. She was unconscious down in that hole and the paramedics had to be called. Once they checked her out, she was okay, the only thing damaged was her pride, she had plenty of soreness to last her and give her something to think about; but her pride ultimately took the death blow.

# <u>Lord, Let's Eat</u>

We finally made it to the hall to have dinner, it was refreshing that it was calm, I couldn't stand another moment of drama.  Sharif and I naturally were side by side coming in, I was really quiet because I was actually pissed, pissed to find out that Ty had been sleeping with Nati, before, during and after our involvement.  Then to learn that Sharif has had sexual relations with her as well, this is way too much.  But now is not the time to address it!  When I see my parents, they motion for me to come over, as Sharif and I reach their table they ask, "How's Topaz?" I replied, "I'm fine, I didn't allow that madness get to me. Besides, time and place - I would never embarrass myself that way." Sharif said, "I'm really sorry about all of that stuff, she is a bit of a problem for our family, most of the time." Mama J smugly said, "I see." I cut that short and said, "Okay I'm going to sit with Sharif and eat is that okay." Whalid interrupted, "Why don't you sit over here with your own family T, we would like to spend a little time with you, we would like to make sure that you are truly fine." I said, "I'm good thank you, but we will have plenty of time to spend with each other." Sharif said, "I don't want to be a problem, I know I have been leaning on him a lot, he has been really good with me through this process, I couldn't have made it without him." Mama J chimed in, "Sharif, there is no problem, take Topaz over to the family table with you, we told you two to lean on each other to make it through this, and you've done a great job." Christine said, "I agree Mrs. Jesper, I couldn't hold back my tears when Topaz went up to sing. I seen how Sharif went up and stood in the gap as support, it was a beautiful thing to see in such a time of need. And Topaz, man when you opened your mouth and sang, I was blown away." I said, "Thank you Christine, I appreciate that." Mama J said, "I was very proud, and not just of my baby, I was proud of you Sharif and your parents; your parents have become like my own children. I'm am so proud of how you guys have conducted yourselves in the face of extreme, and I do mean extreme adversity." She stood from her seat and walked over and embraced Sharif, she said, "Well done Son, I know you wanted to snap, but you held it together and kept your family's dignity intact, the few little things that were said, were said, but it could've been really bad had you not shown some self-control, and you held it together, well done." Sharif responded, "Thank you, I appreciate everything you've done Mrs. J." The two of us went over to the Rudolphson family table and took a seat and quietly awaited the pastor to open the fellowship ceremony.

There were tons of people there, as we sat and ate our food, there were people coming up to the family table and announcing that they would be leaving and giving well wishes to the Rudolphsons. A lot of the people gave me compliments on my singing, it got to be a little embarrassing, just because of the occasion, it wasn't a concert, it was a funeral. I just had a hard time wrapping my head around compliments from something you did at a funeral. The hall that the dinner was held at was a beautiful and nice sized building with lots of rooms for conferences and such; very easy to get lost in. It was roughly around 4:30pm and Sharif and I were standing on the left side of the ballroom when Whalid approached us and asked had we seen Jeremi. He and Christine and our parents were ready to leave, Sharif said, "Did you check outside man, I seen him talking with some of my cousin's; check outside." Whalid said, "Cool, I'm gonna get him and then we will all be ready." He was looking at me, I said, "What does that have to do with me." He said forcefully, "I said, we will ALL be ready to go!" I said, "Whatever Whalid, you need to pump your brakes and go find you delinquent monster and go on home." He stormed out of the ballroom, I told Sharif, "Let's help him find that messy lil' child so they can go, he is getting on my nerves." We walked all over the hall looking, there was no sight of Jeremi anywhere, as we returned to the ballroom there was one small conference room around the corner, as we passed I thought I heard talking, I noticed the light on as we went by it the first time, I said, "Rif," and I pointed at the door as I approached and put my ear to the door, shocked at what I heard. Soft grunting and groaning, I made Sharif listen, he immediately had a big Kool-Aid grin on his face. We turned the knob softly and entered the room, I almost threw up my dinner at the sight of the mess in front of me. Sharif softly closed the door and we entered, we both stood quietly and just watched as Jeremi hovered over the male form sprawled out on the table and used every inch of his throat to get to a happy ending. He was so involved that they didn't even notice us, I was trying to make out who it was lying on the table when I heard the twang in the voice as the figure pushed Jeremi's head into his groin and said, "Suck my shit, you nasty fuckin' fag." Jeremi began to gag, as he seemed to be enjoy himself even more. Sharif blurted out, "How nasty is he Tony?" Sharif approached the edge of the table as Tony sat straight up, almost snapping Jeremi's neck. Sharif continued, "What was all those questions and bullshit about nigga, and then you're up in here straight up gettin' some dome from this little ass boy, and calling him nasty, you're the nasty nigga Tone." Jeremi jumped in, "I'm not no little boy, I bet I can make you cum harder than that Bitch you got with you." I said, "What are you saying you little idiot. You don't even know what you're doing, you are always so willing to give yourself to people who care nothing about you. This boy was in here calling you all out of your name, does he even know your name? Dumb ass!" Tony climbed down off of the table and stood in front of Sharif pleading, "Please don't tell nobody cuzzo, I just wanted to try it and see what was up with it. I was…" At that moment Whalid burst in the door and seen us all standing there, he closed the door behind him and said, "What the fucks up!" Tony got very nervous and continued trying to explain, "I was outside and he rolled up on me and told me I was sexy and looked like I had a big dick. I was thrown off at first but then I figured this is my opportunity to try this thing out. I mean he kinda threw his self at me." Whalid said, "So you just took it upon yourself to put your dick up in my son's mouth! Punk I'll break your Bama-ass neck." Tony didn't back down, he said, "Oh don't sleep me playa, your fuckin' fag came up on me, and I gave him the dick because he asked for it, and he liked it. So if you want to rumble, we can do that nigga!" Jeremi stood in between the two of them and said, "Whalid, you ain't my fuckin' dad, your ass is just jealous and you were staring me down country boy, you wanted this mouth bad and you know it!" Whalid snatched Jeremi by the back of his shirt like a cat, he struggled to get loose and said, "Get the fuck off of me, you bastard!" Whalid yelled, "I'm so sick of you and your bullshit, you don't know when to stop, you're a fuckin' slut, a little slut!" Tony said, "I'm outta here, this shit's crazy!" Jeremi said, "Hey, I definitely wanna finish what we started, I bet your nut tastes so good." We all just looked with our eyes and mouths open in reference to how out of order Jeremi was. Tony was standing in shock as Whalid said, "Oh really, you want this nigga to bust in yo' throat, is that what you're saying?" Jeremi didn't even hesitate when he answered, "I sure do!" Whalid turned to Tony and said, "Pull yo' shit out nigga!" Tony just looked at Whalid, and Whalid said again, "Pull out yo' shit lil' nigga!" Tony said, "What the hell are you talking about my dude, I'm not gonna do that." Whalid responded, "Why not, before we came in you had him suckin yo' shit, didn't you? Go ahead and finish it, it's what my son wants and I get upset when he doesn't get what he wants." Within seconds Jeremi was unzipping Tony's trousers and taking him into his mouth, Sharif grabbed my hand and we exited the room, Whalid stood and watched them, I was appalled. Sharif and I went back to the ballroom just like we didn't know what was going on, we decided to mind our business and not get involved. About 5 minutes later we saw Whalid come and get Christine and head out of the ballroom. I said, "Oh my gosh, we have to follow them Rif, we really shouldn't have left Tony, Whalid may actually beat him up or something, I never know what he's got up his sleeve, we really shouldn't have just left him, come on." We followed them, they went back to the conference room, as we hit the bend to reach the conference room I heard a screech. It was Christine, she said, "What the fuck is this!" As we stepped into the room we could see Tony withdrawing himself from Jeremi and climbing off of him as Jeremi was totally on all fours on top of the table. Jeremi had such a look of shock and betrayal on his face as Whalid screamed at Christine, "This is bullshit, I bring you two with me to something with my family and this is what I get, get your muthafuckin' son man. If he's gonna be gay that's not a problem but to embarrass my family in this way, what the fuck!" Whalid stormed out of the room. Sharif and I stood there as Tony straightened his clothing and eased out of the room and Christine dug straight into Jeremi, "We came here to eat and you got your ass up on a table with a nigga fucking you in yo' ass, are you serious! What is this Jeremi, what is this!" She had tears flowing like a river, it was amazing that she had no inclination that her son was at least bi-sexual, you could hear the hurt in her voice, I felt really bad for her. Jeremi, who is usually full of nasty things to say, was absolutely quiet and looked as if he was just about heartbroken, the betrayal that Whalid had just descended upon him, was to me, unimaginable. Before long Whalid and both my parents had returned to the conference room, Sharif gave me a look and I understood exactly what he was thinking - Uh, oh what next?  Christine continued with her rant, "No son of mine is going to do this, do you understand, you're a god-damned fag!"  She started banging him in his head and in his back as he curled up in a ball on the floor.  She shouted, "Faggot, faggot, faggot!"  Over and over as she banged on him, eventually my dad restrained her and said, "Christine, no baby, this is not the way, trust me, you have to calm down, time will help to heal you both, we will figure this out as a family!"  She pushed my dad away with immense force and said, "Fuck that, I don't ever want to see that freak again!  Don't you ever come anywhere near me ever again!!!!!!"  Sharif and I went over to help Jeremi up off of the floor, he lashed out at us and said, "Don't touch me!  Fuck all of you motherfuckers!  I hope you all die!!!!!!"  He stormed out of the conference room running top speed.  Mama J tried to talk to Christine, "She said Chris please calm down, just let us take Jeremi with us for a few days until this wave of anger moves and we will help you, we are family we can rise through any trial."

She looked Mama J right in her face and said, "What!
Do you think I want a ridiculous spoiled little faggot
like you have.  Hell no, faggots are disgusting, and
all those who love them are disgusting.  If I knew he
was going to be gay, I would have aborted him!  I
don't ever want to see him again, he is dead to me!"

Mama J slowly backed away from Christine and said,
"How could a mother; any mother, say that about her
child – and he is your only child, my God!"  Christine
said, "Fuck you, faggot lovers, I've had enough!"
Whalid had tears in his eyes as he said, "Get away
from here Bitch, and don't you ever speak to my
parents that way, and disrespect my family – go be a
mother to your son.  I don't ever want to see either
of you again, you tacky motherfuckers!"  She said, "To
hell with you, you were almost perfect but you
unfortunately stand behind this sissy as well, I'm
glad I don't have to pretend anymore, everytime he's
around, I itch!"  She stormed out of the room.  We
stayed in the room for about 15 minutes to collect
ourselves before my parents headed home.  I told them
I would be there shortly, I stayed for a moment to
talk to Sharif, we were both in awe of the performance

given by Whalid; the tears and how he was supposedly so embarrassed. And Sharif doesn't even know the half of it. It is amazing to me that someone can be so vindictive and so calculated. He literally destroyed two lives and all lines of communication without blinking an eye, and worked it so well that he ended up looking like the victim, when this was absolutely so far from the truth. That is a testament of how scary some people truly are.

## Got A Lot To Learn

After the day's events I was really drained; physically and emotionally. Once we got home I took off my clothes, showered and went directly to bed; I was sleeping like a rock when I heard my signal for a text message coming through my cell phone. I grabbed my phone and there were sixteen texts from Whalid, I was thinking, 'What the hell, what could he possibly think I want to hear from him.'  The last message read…

Boo-Bear R U up?

It was now 1:30 a.m. and I was more than a little irritated with his position and his performance.  I called him and he immediately answered, "Hey Baby, how ya feelin', I know you've had a rough day."  I replied, "I beg your pardon."  He said, "C'mon, don't be like that, we need to get back to basics, everything that made you unhappy I've gotten rid of. So you need to let me make things right, you know I love you don't you?"  I responded, "Are you crazy?  Or is it that you think I'm crazy, everything you did was done solely for you, it had nothing to do with me. You set Jeremi up and left him in a position where nobody trusts anything he says and his mother basically hates him, that was so cold blooded." Whalid stopped me, "No T, that wasn't my intention, I did expose him to Christine, but I didn't know she would trip like that over his homosexuality.  She pissed me off saying that bullshit about you, I was ready to choke her, she's done, I'll never speak to that hoe again." I said, "Why not, she didn't say anything worse than you've said to me lately." He said, "Stop it, don't say that, I am truly sorry about everything that I did and said." I said, "Man, all that shit you did…" he said, "But listen, just hear me out; the stuff with Ty was bad, but you heard it today, he was cheating on you all along with Nati." I replied, "I don't want to get into the me and Tylique situation, whatever he did, doesn't matter anymore, I have forgiven him. Know that. Now you, you are still here, the forgiveness is quite a bit more difficult." The line was quiet for a moment and then Whalid said, "I don't want to argue with you Boo-Bear, what can I do to get you back? Do you want me to buy you something, do you want me to take you somewhere. Tell me, if you give me a chance I put my tongue anywhere you want it, I miss our sex sessions, I know you do to. My dick aches for you, I got a hard on right now just thinking about your smooth skin and the tightness of your…" I interrupted him, "Whalid, sex with you is the absolute last thing on my mind, trust me. I don't need gifts, trips or anything, I just need to be left alone. Can't we just be cordial, and be brothers which is legally what we are, nothing more." He snapped, "I don't have any muthafuckin' brothers, you are my… you are the love of my life T, don't you know that? But see I think I know what the problem is, it's that nigga wit' the braids, I ain't playin' this game, I'll take that nigga down about you T." I said, "What the hell are you talking about?" He yelled, "That fuckin' Sharif, don't play you know what I'm talkin' about! If I find out that nigga been up in you, I'ma fuck both of y'all up!" I said, "Threats, threats, threats, cut it out, ass-jack. Stop always threatening folks. And why would you think that something was going on with me and Sharif, and more importantly, what business of yours is it?" Whalid added, "I could see the way he was all over you, like you were one of his hoes. Everytime you move, he moves – everywhere you're at, he's at. I'm not feelin' it, and I'm telling you now, if it is going on, then end it immediately. I paused for a moment and then I said, "Hey you, with the dreads and the bad attitude, who are you to tell me when to end and begin and with whom, you need to pump your brakes dude, seriously." He replied, "All I'm sayin' is, if I catch that corny ass nigga dippin' in my shit, he is going to pay. So you can end it now and save him the ass-whoopin'." I replied, "Stop accusing me of things and being in my business, and stop thinking that you can just go up and whoop people's ass, you can't beat everybody. One of these times somebody's gonna bust you in your shit and then what." He chuckled and replied, "There ain't never been but one nigga that bust me in my shit and that was you last week, and you better never make the mistake again." I said, "What the hell ever, you better never say what you said to me again or guess what, I'm gonna crash you again tough guy." He laughed out loud, "T you got some shit wit' you. But I just can't shake you, you do something to me. When you're not around I can't get you off my mind. Since the first time we had sex anytime my shit get stiff you come to mind, it drives me crazy. It doesn't even matter who I'm with it's you that I want to sex." I interrupted him, "Okay Boy, I get it, you can stop now, you're talking crazy." He replied, "No I'm not and I'm not exaggerating, if you could experience how it is to run all up in your guts, Oh my God! Boo-Bear you just don't know - Whoa! You got my shit on brick right now. Let me come and get you right now, you don't have to stay all night if you don't want to, but I wish you would. I promise, no arguing, no complaining, and no fighting - just me up in yo' shit all night. Mmmmm, I can't wait to bust all up in yo' shit." I was literally squirming in my seat, I can't stand the fact that he has some type of a hold on me, but I just cant seem to shake it. It's like he knows just what to say and when, it is so aggravating to me. I took a deep breath and said, "Whalid, I can't - I can't come over there, it's not a good idea." He came back with, "Well, how 'bout I come over there." I said, "What is that, I have no say or control over that, but I'm not having sex with you." He said, "That's fine, then when I get there don't have sex with me, I didn't have anything that nice in mind anyway, I'd rather you fuck my brains out." I tried catching myself but I ended up laughing and saying, "No Whalid, nothing at all." He said, "I can't believe you are so heartless, your gonna make me injure myself, how can you be so heartless?" I laughed and just as I was feeling myself weakening by the moment, his phone beeped with an incoming call, subsequently killing the mood immediately. I said, "Look, you're in luck. Some trick heard your wounded cry. It was nice talking to you Bro, I'm signing off, I'll speak to ya soon." He began to try to explain, "No Baby, this is Chris, she's trippin, I ain't even gonna answer her. I don't want nothin' to do wit' that bitch ever!" I said, "I understand Whalid and I'm not questioning you, I'm just all wiped out and I need to get some sleep, that's all." He said, "T seriously Baby, are you mad?" I said, "That's so silly, why would I be mad about your phone ringing Whalid, that has nothing to do with me, it's none of my business." He pleaded, "Please don't hang up T," I said, "I'm sleepy, what do you want me to sit here and start snoring in your ear?" He said, "Okay can I call you tomorrow?" I said, "What's stopping you?" He said, "Hey T," I said, "Yes Whalid," his voice deepened and he declared, "I love the shit outta you Boo." I paused and said, "I know you do."

When I woke up it was 11:22am I had all intentions on being up and moving around by 9am. I went and checked my cell phone, it was beeping, letting me know there was a new voicemail waiting. I listened to the voicemail as I sat at the edge of my bed…

Hello Topaz, this is Sam, I am your sister TriAnn's fiancé and I would love to speak to you about a few things that are really important. Please gimme a call back at 412-444-7088. Thanks.

I just sat there for a moment with the obvious questions running through my head. What, why and how in the hell did you get my number? I sat for a moment and then I decided to call the number back to see what he wanted. After three rings he answered, "Yo, this is Sam!" I replied, "Hi Sam, this is Topaz, I got your message, whassup." He cleared his throat and began, "Hey Lil dude, I wanted to talk to you, I don't know if you know it or not, but your sister and I are engaged to be married in a few months. And you are the one person in the family that I haven't had the pleasure of spending any time with, and being as though we are gonna be brothers, I would like to sit down with you briefly, just so you can get to know me a little and vice versa. I don't want to build a relationship on what someone says, I like to draw my own conclusions about folks, ya feel me." I laughed and said, "Wow, is my family still bad mouthing me that intensely?" He said, "No, nothing like that, I just wanna meet you for myself, I won't take up a lot of your time, can you just give me about 30 minutes or so, cause there's another situation I want to discuss with you as well." I said, "That's fine, when did you want to do this because I will be leaving here to go back to school shortly." He said, "ASAP, do you have some time this afternoon?" I replied, "That actually is the only time I have, I wanna be out of here by at least six o'clock." He said, "That's cool, I can come see you now if that's okay, I am close to where you stay." I said, "How do you… nevermind." I gave him the address and he said, "Cool Lil dude, I'll see ya in about twenty." I said, "No problem." We hung up and I was feeling a little uneasy, but I figured it was just me, there is no telling what the Bailleau clan has told this man about me, it kind of makes me nervous.

There is one more conversation that I must have before I leave, and that is with Sharif. I sent him a text message that said…

I need to see you before I leave here, I'm leaving at

      six.  It's important; I'll be at home.

     I got myself together, I was wearing an outfit
fit for a two hour drive, I needed to be comfortable.
I had on a red body glove top with no sleeves and a
pair of oversized red Nike sweatpants, and red and
white Nike sneakers.  I was in my room getting my
things together when I heard the door bell ringing.  I
ran down the stairs and walked toward the door, as I
looked out of the glass I could see it was Sam, I
opened the door and looked him over as he stood there.
He was an average looking dude with caramel skin, he
stood about 5 foot 11 inches tall, his body was pretty
solid, but he didn't have a lot of muscle definition,
like I said, he was just average.  His best attribute
would have to be his hazel eyes, they were pretty
bright.  He was wearing a really nice Nike sweatsuit,
he said, "Hey lil dude, can I come in."  I chuckled
and said, "Come on.  Would you like something to
drink?"  He said, "Sure," I gave him a orange soda
from the fridge and told him to have a seat.  He
started the conversation, "Let's get right to it, I'm
gonna be marrying your sister in about 6 weeks and I

would like for every member of your family to be there." I laughed and said, "Surely you are here without consulting TriAnn, there's just one small problem with your plan, TriAnn hates my guts and I'm really not all that fond of her. There's no real reason to ruin her wedding day with my presence." He replied, "See that's what I'm talking about, y'all gots to let that go, y'all are family and you can't change that," I said, "Nor have I tried; I was taken by a foster family due to my birth family's physical and verbal abuse. Is that the story their telling or have they made up something else to tell folks?" He responded, "I try not to deal in those types of things, I am not really a total part of the family yet, so I really have no place to discuss such things. The reason I'm here is all selfish, it's about what I want." He chuckled and continued, "I want you and I to be on good terms. I think you are a cool Lil dude, and I hope you don't mind me calling you Lil dude." I smiled and said, "Not really, those are just the facts, I am little, I can't do anything about that." He smiled wide and showed a mouth full of gorgeous, white, well-kept teeth as he continued, "I want you to sing at my wedding." I was taken aback, I said, "You must not have talked to TriAnn about that, I know she would die if she even knew you were having these thoughts." He said, "One thing about me," as he stood and walked toward me, "I know how to get what I want. Very seldom do I hear the word No." He was now standing directly in front of me staring intensely into my eyes as he continued, "Know what I mean. I can imagine that you don't hear NO very much either." I played coy just like I wasn't following his conversation, I said, "What makes you say that Sam?" He said, "Don't play, you know as well as I do what you have working in your favor," the Kool-Aid grin returned to his face. "You are totally spoiled, and everybody around you treats you like a little girl, they are all at your beacon call. Your ex-boyfriend's parents and his brother - Whalid and his parents, your Uncle Joe, just everybody; they all seem to make sure you have what you need." I said, "Yes, I guess you're right on one hand, but on the other hand my mother and my sister could care less if I drop dead today." He grabbed me in an awkward embrace and said, "That's part of why I'm here, I want to put an end to all that, as soon as possible. I can't stand family issues, they are really draining." His arms were resting at my shoulders and he was looking down at me. I said, "Really, so how is that little family tift between TriAnn and my mom concerning who was going to end up with you, because the last I heard they were fist fighting." He said, "Not to worry, they are cordial. Your mom will even be at the wedding. So wassup, are you gonna be a good brother-in-law to me or what? Can't we all just get along?" He then swiftly slid his hands down and rested them on my behind, I looked up in his face and there was that dumb ass grin, I said, "So what you want is cooperation the whole way around, you want every family member to service you however you see fit." He responded, "No, it's not that, I just want our lives to be easy." I said, "I hope you don't think this bullshit is a good definition of easy, it seems more like you are trying to make a dick hungry slut out of me. Why would I want to (air quotes) cooperate with you in this manner, when you've already had cooperation from my sister and my mom? That ain't cool Sam." He said, "Trust me it'll be cool, y'all don't even see each other enough for anyone to catch on, and real talk," he grabbed my hand and placed it on his totally erect penis, "It's ecstasy. I puts it down with this snake." I immediately broke contact with him and said, "Okay, enough already, I don't like where this is going…" he interrupted, "If you just chill right quick, all this snake could be goin' in your mouth." I was getting really irritated, I snapped, "First of all, you keep talking about snakes and I really don't like reptiles, and second, you're offering a snake and all I felt was an average garden worm – the one thing I hate even more than reptiles is false advertisement. Did you know you could be sued for that?" He stepped back as his eyebrows rose far up his forehead and he yelled, "Aw Bitch, you ain't all that now and your mouth is a little too smart for you to be so little." I said, "Don't call me out of my name punk ass and what does my size have to do with anything; you wouldn't be up in my house trying to threaten me would you, short dick?" His eyes were growing kind of wide as he responded, "I'm not threatening anybody, I'm just saying, you talk a lot of shit for a nigga that let other niggas run up in him.  I'm positive, you'll be sprung on this dick just like your sister is."  I leaned my head to the side slightly and said, "Surely if you were paying any attention you would've noticed that my sister and I – Ah, no comparison, we are like night and day in most ways."  He replied, "I know and you got a fat ass and I want some."  I said, "Well that's not possible."  He combated, "Why not?"  I smiled and said, "Let's just start with anatomy," he had a look of confusion come over his face as he said, "What?"  I said, "The person with the biggest piece gets to be the top; that means I'm winning."  He said, "Your mouth makes me want to slap you then kiss the fuck outta you."  He grabbed me tight and started trying to bite my neck, I was struggling to get loose when I heard the door bell ring, I was so relieved.  I broke free and headed for the front door.  As I reached the door and opened it I was never so happy to see Sharif ever.  As he entered the doorway he immediately seen Sam coming up the hallway and I watched as he eyebrows rolled up into the "I have an **ATTITUDE**" range, he said, "Wassup Luv?"  I said, "Oh wow, long story – I am so happy to see you, I thought you were gonna miss me, I'll be out of here soon." Sam said, "Wassup man," as he shook Sharif's hand. Sharif reluctantly responded, "Sup." As he stepped onto the porch Sam said, "We can finish this another time Lil dude, I'm not giving up on you." I said, "Why do I believe that?" Sharif abruptly said, "Yeah alright, later for all that," as he pulled me in the house and slammed the door. He started in on me, "What the fuck is that, what was that lame doin' over here?" I said, "Easy there buddy! He actually came to ask me to sing at him and TriAnn's wedding and…" he cut me off and blurted out, "And what else? He was all grinned up and shit – wit' that ole, we can continue – blah – fuck him!" I said, "Hey stop it right now and have a seat, I want to discuss something really important with you, have a seat." He walked into the livingroom and sat down on the couch. I walked over and sat next to him on the couch, he stopped me and threw a strange look my way, I said, "What's that about!" He said, "My point exactly, I sat here waiting on you to lap up and you sit next to me. Then this little stuff with ole boy, c'mon I'm starting to get heated." I got up and sat on his lap and said, "Better." He said, "Absolutely," I started in, "Okay Rif, we have to talk, I'm leaving at six o'clock to go back to school, but there's some things that I want to tie up before I go." He wrapped his arms around my waist and said, "What do you mean tie up, Luv?" I continued, "Last night I had some time to really reflect on my position, and I don't like where I'm at. Usually I see my life going in a direction that is not beneficial for me and I get so caught up with the actual situation itself that I just continue and then I have a very hard time once everything is all out of wack. Well, I'm not doing it this time; I refuse." He said, "Did I do something?" I said, "Well yes and no." Silence entered the room and Sharif just had his face resting against my back. I continued, "There was so much that went on this week that it was hard to take it all in, but like I said, last night I got a chance to really process what has been said and done. The biggest thing that has stuck out for me is the situation with Nati, you and Ty. You have literally stated that you and Ty were sleeping with Nati, that really bothered me." He lifted his head and said, "Why does that bother you?" I got up off of his lap and stood in front of him and

said, "I beg your pardon, are you serious?" He was
just sitting there with a puzzled look on his face, I
could feel myself becoming very irritated. I think he
noticed my irritation and figured he better start
talking, he started, "That was before you and I did
anything." I yelled, "Rif, that is not the point. You
slept with your brother's girlfriend while they were
together and then you continued after they broke up.
How do you know the baby isn't yours instead of Ty's?"
He snapped, "You sound like my mom wit' that bullshit.
She's talking about we need to get a blood test." I
said, "She is right, that little girl has the right to
know if you are actually her uncle or her father, and
you should want to know, what's wrong with you Sharif.
I don't understand, do you have any feelings for Nati
at all?" He said, "None, she is a decent piece of ass
and that's all." Silence fell, I couldn't move, and I
couldn't say anything, I was appalled. He said,
"C'mon, sit back down LT." I said, "Not, this is it,
this is where I get off. I see where this is going to
go and I refuse to lose you like this, I'd rather give
you up now and cut my losses." He stood up and
grabbed me by my arms and said, "Ain't nobody leavin'

nobody! I'm not goin' let you leave me like that." I said, "You don't have any other choice, Sharif I can't go down that road with you. Ty cheated for the whole relationship and now that is evident and been proven, I forgave him and I let it go. What I'm not going to do is go into a relationship with you having to forgive you for things and questioning your motives right from the very beginning. I can't - I'm sorry, I just can't." He fired back at me, "You aren't totally innocent now, I came in here today and…" I cut him right off, "Stop, we're not doing it. You know nothing was going on, but if it had, wouldn't I be right in line with your bullshit. So let's not bullshit each other and let's be to each other, what we've been a system of support and back up. I need my friend Sharif right now, nothing else. Can you do that?" He looked very deflated as he answered, "I guess I have no other choice." I tried to fight it but one tear rolled down my face, he grabbed me and kissed me deeply, I gave in to the kiss, and I knew that was the last time. He broke the kiss and grabbed my face and said, "I do love you LT and I'm never gonna give up on what we have, but I won't force you."

He kissed my forehead and headed out the front door, and to my surprise I actually broke down in tears sitting there on the couch. I guess I was a little more invested than I thought.

Once I pulled myself together I packed my things in my jeep and sat down in the gameroom until my parents got home, they were running a little late, but I wouldn't dare leave without them seeing me off. While I was waiting I called Akai to thank her and the girls for coming and supporting me in my time of need. The funniest thing was when she told me that she didn't want to laugh but the whole episode with Nati taking the plunge into the grave site was caught on someone phone and had been placed on Facebook and YouTube. She said it was ridiculous how many hits and comments were listed about it, I found it quite amusing myself. She also shared that there were clips of me singing at church and folks had made a lot of positive comments on those clips as well. Now that was a little weird, because I really have no interest in seeing that or reliving any of that, it was just too painful. I hung up with Akai, and told her I'd see her shortly, I could hear Mama and Papa J coming

in the front door.  I met them in the hallway and told
them that I had decided to get on my way back to
school and I had been waiting on them.  They sat me
down to make sure that my mind was in the right space
to take the drive alone and they let me know as usual
how much they loved me and told me to call as soon as
I got there.  We said our goodbyes and I jumped in my
jeep and I was on my way.  I was only a little behind
my original departure time I set, it was about 6:45pm.
As I pulled away from the house I immediately noticed
Sharif's Cadillac tailing behind me, within moments my
cell phone rang.  I answered and said, "Yes Mr.
Rudolphson," he said, "I knew you were just waiting
for your parents, I've been at the top of the street
waiting so that I could see you off.  I told you, I'm
not giving up on you, not just yet.  And for the
record, the ass, that's mine, I definitely won't be
allowing anyone to get close to that."  I said, "Rif,
we are not going there, and nobody's trying to get at
me and I'm not trying to let anybody get at me, I want
to be by myself, seriously, I don't need all the
complications."  He replied, "Well when you are ready,
I'll still be here waiting, period.  I'm not going

away, done deal. I'm going to hang up Luv. I'm going to follow you to the interstate to see you off, please text me as soon as you pull up in front of your apartment, will you do that?" I said, "Yes Sharif," he said, "I love you LT!" I felt my body tense up as I fought back tears and listened to the phone line disconnect. He continued tailing me to the interstate just like he said and as he turned off and I no longer seen his car a tear escaped and ran down my cheek. I know he's not good for me but it is so hard to cut him off, but I know it is what needs to be done.

About twenty minutes into my drive my phone rang, I thought it was Sharif, I didn't even look at the caller id when I answered, "Wassup." I heard, "Damn did you know it was me," I took a pause, because at first I didn't catch the voice. Then I caught that it was Whalid, I lied and said, "Of course I knew it was you." He said, "Usually you answer like you hate me and I'm getting on your nerves. When you just answered you sound like the love of my life." I said, "Whatever Boy," he said, "Mom told me you were on your way back to school, I would've really like to have seen you before you left but that's okay. If you ever give me permission, I will drive up to see you when you have some time." I just didn't say anything, he said, "Boo-Bear are you there?" I said, "Yes, I hear you, we will see, I really have to concentrate on me, I'm gonna be so far behind, but we'll see what happens." He said, "I'll accept that. Hey T," I said, "Yes," he said, "I love the shit outta you Boy, and I'll never let go of what we have! Text me and let me know they you made it home safely, will you do that Boo?" I said, "I will."

When it comes to the men in my life, my words seem to fall on deaf ears. And I believe it's because my actions don't always match. I'm getting stronger but I know I have a lot to learn yet when it comes to matters of the heart.

As I made my way back toward Jackson College I sat and thought to myself, 'Let's try this again!' My first week being enrolled in college was not at all what I'd expected. Though I've learned more in this past week than any other. The funniest thing is I have yet to attend one college class - how is that possible! My gosh, this is a crazy life, what's next!

And do I really want to know!!!!!

# THE END

Make sure you also read...

## Loving Topaz

and

## Losing Topaz

*Thank you for your continued support of this series*